Something about a house is different when there's another person breathing in it. As soon as I stepped through the door, I knew someone was in the house. Something was different. A smell, a sound, the absence of an expected sound, something.

When I set it down, the bag from the thrift shop made a crinkling sound that seemed alarmingly loud. I moved stealthily toward the kitchen and quietly slid a knife from the drawer. I checked that my phone was in my pocket.

No one was on the first floor; that was evident. If anyone was upstairs, he or she was at a decided disadvantage. I stood still and raised my eyes to the loft railing. Nothing. No sign of movement.

I began the slow, silent climb up the stairs, staying on the outside edge where squeaks were less likely. A shudder ran down my arms, lifting the hair, holding up the fabric of my shirt like a picnic cloth on dry grass. When my eyes were level with the loft floor, I surveyed the room.

Someone was in the bed.

Same River Twice

by

Janet Poland

Same River Twice

Cover Art by *RJ Morris*

The Wild Rose Press, Inc.
PO Box 708
Adams Basin, NY 14410-0708
Visit us at www.thewildrosepress.com

Publishing History
First Mainstream Thriller Edition, 2018
Print ISBN 978-1-5092-2117-2
Digital ISBN 978-1-5092-2118-9

Published in the United States of America

Acknowledgments

You never know where a story is going to come from. I once had a temporary job drawing little dots on maps to indicate where scientists had collected specimens of fungi in the Rocky Mountains. As I performed this laborious work, I dreamed up a mystery plot in which fungi would play a role. And here we are.

It helped that I have a dear friend, Amy Rossman, PhD, who generously enlightened me about the amazing world of fungi.

My friend Ann J. Kirschner was kind enough to read the manuscript when it hadn't quite found its footing. Her wise insights and suggestions helped get it up and running.

I appreciate the contributions of my editor at The Wild Rose Press, Anne Duguid Knol, whose eagle eye caught errors and suggested worthy improvements.

And finally, I must thank my husband, Gary Blackburn, who cheered me on from beginning to end.

Chapter One

My hands were tied behind my back, so I had to pull the panel closed with my feet. I was in total darkness, in a space just big enough to hold a seated person. There wasn't room to stand. Someone had made this space, had hollowed out the side of the massive fireplace, then split the stones to veneer and fitted them onto a hinged panel.

I couldn't tell if the panel had latched behind me. It had been used—or at least intended—to conceal someone who was being hunted.

Like me.

I wondered what had become of whoever had hidden here, more than one hundred and fifty years ago. Were they trapped? They must have gotten out, or the space would be full of bones.

Then I thought, how do I know it isn't full of bones?

Tires crunched on the gravel drive outside. But the sound faded.

I was on my own.

Then a closer sound: a whiny, querulous voice. Slightly muffled, but I heard panic through the stone.

"Miren?"

A pause, then louder.

"Miren!"

I stopped my lungs as long as I could. There was

1

breathing right outside the panel. In the fireplace. When I inhaled, I caught the faint odor of lamp oil and soot. Then, the grind of the damper, stiff with rust, and the slight patter of residue as it dropped onto the flagstone hearth. I pictured the oil lamp, held aloft. Now my name came from very close, from higher up, in the base of the flue.

"Miren?"

Footsteps. Close, then distant. Back and forth. Hurried. A disorganized search. They became fainter, then stopped. I was alone, undetected. For now. I got to work on the knot behind me.

Time went by. The knot yielded slightly, softening as I wiggled it back and forth. My fingers and wrists were probably bleeding, and I didn't care. And finally, I felt the hard nub of the knot turn into a loop, just big enough to fit my fingers through and pull. More time went by. Finally, the rope fell away. My hands were free. My shoulders resisted as I moved my arms painfully forward and flexed my fingers.

I was afraid to open the panel. Who would I find outside? How long could I wait, without food or water? Should I try to escape while I had the advantage of darkness?

I thought back to how it all started. It seemed so routine, in retrospect. That day at *The Bucks County Clarion* when everyone worried about their jobs as newsroom positions evaporated.

Back then, I was afraid of losing my job.

Now I was afraid of dying.

****

The ax fell on Friday.

We arrived in the newsroom that August morning

to find security guards stationed at pivotal points along the corridors.

Then the phones rang, one by one, as editors and reporters were summoned to the office.

None returned.

As the newsroom thinned out, dread and apprehension settled over us like a storm cloud. I was on automatic pilot, finishing a lightweight story about an antique car show in New Hope. I searched the cloud for silver linings, but it wasn't easy. I needed this job. I needed my own place, my independence.

I sent my file to the features desk and contemplated those silver linings. I didn't have a mortgage. No kids or pets depended on me. I'd been through worse, and I'd get through this.

And then my turn came. I stood before F.X. Rosenzweig, harried and gray in his shirtsleeves. He motioned me to a chair. "We appreciate all you've done for the *Clarion* over the past year, Miren. Unfortunately, our profit paradigm is such that the mission can no longer sustain our current level of..." His voice trailed off.

He waved his hands in a you-get-my-drift motion and sighed. "We're reducing the newsroom staff by a third. I'm told it's still possible to put out a paper, but we'll have to do more with less, as they say."

He shuffled through a nest of folders on his desk. "Lassiter, Lassiter...here it is. You will receive severance based on years of service, which in your case will amount to—oh dear."

I know, I thought. Bupkis and change.

"You moved here from out West last year to take this job, didn't you? I'm sorry it didn't last longer."

F.X. wiped a faint sheen of sweat from above his lip. He sank back in his chair.

"So, do you think you'll stay around here? Or go back to Nevada? I gather you have family out there?"

I tried to stay calm on the outside, but inwardly, I bristled. I am thirty-eight years old, and even if I still had family there, which I did not, did he expect me to hitchhike in defeat back to Elk City and bunk in my old bedroom?

"Actually, Mr. R., I haven't had much time to think about it, since you just fired me a minute ago."

F.X. looked alarmed. "No! Not fired! Laid off."

I wondered briefly if his own job was in danger. I took pity on him. I do this a lot. I really shouldn't.

He ticked off a few more points. He said he would be happy to write a recommendation should I need one. He said my personal effects would be boxed up and available in the lobby. He said I would be escorted out by a security guard. He said he was sorry.

****

I lived in a one-bedroom apartment above a Mr. Bubbles' Coin Laundry in a strip mall a few miles from the *Clarion* building. It was cheap, private, and warm in winter from the endless labors of the washers and dryers downstairs. It was far enough away from the paper that I was spared the likelihood of colleagues dropping by to say hi. I get along fine with my co-workers, but I don't want them showing up unannounced at my door.

I collected the carton of *Clarion* items from the backseat of the Corolla and tossed in the mail from the box near the outer door. I gripped my keys in my teeth for the trip upstairs.

I'm super careful on stairs and with anything that might try to entangle and trip me. I'm tall and hardly delicate, but I have a tendency to get snagged on things. I've performed some remarkable pirouettes and jetés and would prefer not to repeat them.

I made it safely to my apartment, a minimal affair with white walls, beige carpet and a kitchen with home-center cabinets and a breakfast bar. My furniture was a combination of IKEA and items my colleagues had donated to the cause. I didn't need much; as long as I had my laptop, my phone and my stack of library books, I was good.

I dropped the carton on the counter and took out several thick manila envelopes with my clips, a paper copy of every story I'd written over the past year. A pile of amusing headlines with pinholes where I'd posted them on my bulletin board. An award from an allergy association, in the form of a giant dust mite, at roughly 150x magnification.

A coffee mug with "Elk City Rocks!" emblazoned on the side, a souvenir of the Northwest Nevada Rocks and Minerals Association convention. An "Elk City Pride" bumper sticker. A potted cactus named Lance, after a particularly irritating PR flack.

I turned to the mail. Ads for things I was no way interested in: spas, financial planning, cruises, cosmetic surgery, lavish landscaping services. A letter from the property manager of the apartment complex, and a heavy cream-colored envelope with the return address of Baldur, Cresson and Greenwood, Attorneys-at-Law.

First, the landlord.

Dear Tenant:

Due to unanticipated increases in utilities, property

taxes, maintenance, and other outgoes, we regret that as of October 1, your rent will increase to...

I slapped the letter onto the counter. True, no one depended on me, I was tough and independent and all, but still. A layoff and a hefty rent increase in one day?

My tired but comfortable loveseat caught my eye, as did the stack of books on the side table and my laptop on the coffee table. Suddenly the apartment shimmered with precious solitude. I pictured the addition of a sofa bed or futon for the roommate I would be required to take on. I imagined music that involved a lot of screaming, and loud and badly behaved dogs and boyfriends. I vowed I would live in a cardboard box by the railroad tracks, as long as I had that box to myself.

I turned back to the mail and picked up the cream-colored envelope. My address was individually typed, making it less likely to be junk.

A lawsuit, perhaps? That would round things off nicely. But I was quite sure they had to serve subpoenas in person.

It was from one of the law partners listed at the top of the page:

Dear Miss Lassiter:

Allow me to offer my condolences on the death of your great-uncle, Elias Lassiter. As Mr. Lassiter's attorney, I am writing to inform you that you are named as a beneficiary in his last will and testament.

Kindly contact me at the telephone number above at your earliest convenience so that we may expedite the distribution of this estate.

Yours truly,

Edmond L. Greenwood

I'd learned about the death of my father's Uncle Elias a few months ago. Although I'd skipped the memorial meeting at the old Quaker meetinghouse in Whitworth, I'd thought about him warmly.

Uncle Elias was a kindly but reclusive eccentric in a family of kindly eccentrics. He was a botanist, or more accurately, a mycologist, who had trouble focusing on people if there was a fungus in the vicinity. He was a bit odd, but he had been kind to me during his visits to my childhood home when his collecting expeditions brought him to the Great Basin.

And now he'd named me in his will. Not that his estate was likely to amount to much besides cartons of mildew, but you never knew.

I checked my watch. Almost five p.m. I dialed the number of Baldur, Cresson and Greenwood, and reached voice mail. Presumably lawyers keep sensible hours. I left a message.

Now it was after five. I poured myself a healthy glass of wine.

****

On Saturday morning, I boiled water and made cowboy coffee: five heaping spoonfuls in a battered metal pot, set to steep. My mother swore by simple, high plains brew, which she, as the descendant of Basque sheepherders, insisted was best prepared over a campfire. It has a reputation for bitterness, but that's from boiling. To make it right, you boil the water, not the coffee. It's nectar of the gods, with or without a few scoops of plain old white sugar.

When it was ready, I poured a mug and settled down at my desk. I tried to log on to my *Clarion* account and was denied. They'd already erased my identity from cyberspace. Using my personal account, I sent a quick message to Jodi, my editor in the features department, asking if she still had a job.

As soon as I hit send, my phone rang.

"Miss Lassiter? This is Edmond Greenwood, of Baldur, Cresson and Greenwood, returning your call. Thanks for getting in touch with me so quickly."

Greenwood expressed condolences again about Uncle Elias, then turned to the task at hand.

"Ordinarily I'd have you come into the office to go over the terms of your uncle's will, but since the only property he left you was his house and its contents, I thought it might make sense to take you out there and let you see it. I can bring the initial paperwork we'll need to take care of."

House? I had no idea where Uncle Elias had lived, or what kind of house he had. I was intrigued. I kind of needed a house.

"It's in Fenton's Crossing, a bit upriver from your area. Are you familiar with it?"

I was not. Numerous small villages formed a chain of quaintness along the Delaware River, and I'd probably driven through some, but I couldn't remember.

"I often work weekends, but this one is pretty full. May I pick you up Wednesday? I'd like to get moving on probating this portion of your uncle's will, and you really need to see the house. I can assure you you'd never find it on your own."

Uh-oh. Hard to find? A shack hidden in the woods?

I told him I had Wednesday off, which was technically true, and that any time would work. We agreed on ten a.m., and I gave him directions to the apartment.

****

Whether Elias had left me a colonial-era stone mansion—which I doubted—or a shack in the woods, I would have either a place to live if I liked it, or a property to sell if I didn't. Either way, I felt better about the housing situation.

Now to my livelihood. I checked my email and saw that Jodi had responded.

Miren,

I'm so sorry. I'm still the features editor, but I don't know how I'm going to fill the section without a writer. I still have June. I'll have a free-lance budget, so I'll see what I can give you if you're willing. Mark, Jen, Spencer, Kevin, and Carlos are still here. I don't look forward to Monday.

If there's anything I can do, whether it's lending you some dough or recommending you for another job, just let me know.

My spirits rose. With Jodi, such words were meant sincerely.

****

I called Jodi Monday morning. I knew she'd be busy and preoccupied, but I needed to know the status of stories begun and interviews already scheduled. Should I continue with them, and bill them as freelance projects?

She made paper-rustling sounds, and I could picture her at her untidy desk, expertly extracting whatever she needed from a haystack of papers. "Okay. I've got you down for three that were assigned pre-massacre. What I really need is Pleat, with photos, for Sunday. After that, we'll talk."

I'd scheduled an interview for Tuesday morning with Millicent Pleat, the retiring curator of the quirky Mercer Museum in Doylestown. A century ago, an eccentric millionaire named Henry Chapman Mercer had scoured the region collecting pre-industrial tools and craftworks and displayed them as relics of a lost world in his concrete cathedral. Jodi wanted a peek at Pleat and what made her tick, and a look at the Mercer collection itself.

Jodi said she'd schedule the photographer—as a staffer, I would have arranged that myself. She agreed to pay me as a freelancer for the feature and asked for twenty-four inches by Friday morning.

And so it came to pass that the next morning, I headed for Doylestown, the county seat. It's a pleasant town, despite its confusing web of one-way streets that join one another at acute angles. Nineteenth-century brick homes and offices shared space with coffee shops and law firms. I parked next to the old prison, which now houses the Michener Art Museum and its fine collection of New Hope School impressionist paintings.

In the early twentieth century, Mercer spent his life and fortune on a series of castles—all constructed of concrete—in the town. They included his home, Fonthill, and the Moravian Pottery and Tile Works, where his beloved arts-and-crafts style decorative tiles are still produced. The third castle, the Mercer, houses his immense collection of tools and pre-industrial technology.

I gave my name to the woman at the desk, who nodded and reached for the phone. She was middle-aged, and exhibited distinctive grooming, from her golden beehive to her glossy fuchsia fingernails.

Spangly earrings dangled from her earlobes, and her black eyebrows were drawn in dramatically. Each started with a solid circle, then curved in a thin, arched tail, as though two giant sperm cells were preparing to duke it out on her forehead.

A tall, handsome woman with short white hair approached from a hallway and extended her hand. "Miren? Hi, I'm Millicent Pleat. Thanks, Marilyn." She nodded at the receptionist and led me toward the museum doorway.

"We can sit down in my office and chat after I take you on a quick tour of the museum.

"We'll start here and work our way up to the gallows," she said, with a twinkle.

We entered the ground floor and found ourselves in the nave of a cathedral. But instead of saints looking down from the gothic arches and clerestory windows, every possible artifact known to pre-industrial America hung from the walls or was displayed in cases and small rooms like chapels on each level: a stagecoach, a Conestoga wagon, a whaling boat, a hand-pumped fire engine, presses and grinders for every possible fruit or nut. There was equipment for every industry; mining, tanning, printing, blacksmithing. Tools for domestic arts like soap and candle making, butter churning, spinning, weaving, shoemaking,

At this stage, I hardly needed to ask questions. I was madly scribbling Millicent's running commentary, while absorbing impressions as we went along. A key element in a feature story is the telling detail—the small observation that brings the story to life. It might be the costumed historical reenactor checking his cell phone, or the box of baking soda used to freshen the refrigerator where the serial killer has stashed his dismembered victims.

My problem here was an excess of details. I tried to open my observational pores as we wound our way around the open central space, rising from floor to floor,

At the top, the roof closed down toward us as we passed what seemed like hundreds of firebacks, decorative iron panels installed at the backs of fireplaces to reflect heat outward.

The concrete stairs narrowed as we neared the roof, and Millicent gestured me to go ahead to where the museum's more morbid artifacts were housed. I passed the hearse and the prisoner's dock with its sharp iron spikes designed, I imagined, to discourage escape.

I turned the corner and saw the dark rough wood of the scaffold's base. I stopped cold.

Chapter Two

Millicent stumbled into my back. She leaned around me to see why I had stopped in my tracks and clucked her tongue in annoyance. "Now this is not..." she began, in her best Girl Scout leader voice. But then she looked more closely.

A figure in tan slacks hung by a thick rope, with the shoes about eye level. One shoe, more precisely; one was missing and revealed a worn, mustard-colored sock. I doubted that the museum would display a gallows complete with a mannequin to demonstrate its use.

She stepped forward and gasped. "Oh, it's Graham! Oh!" She clambered up the wooden ladder on the side of the gallows to where the rope was knotted cruelly under the man's jaw. Over her shoulder, I could make out his purple distorted face, the mouth open and the swollen tongue extended. He was clearly beyond help.

"Miss Pleat," I cautioned, "we shouldn't touch anything." She didn't hear me. She clung to the ladder, her elegant black heels struggling to keep her feet hooked onto the rungs. She seemed frozen, and I worried that she would slip and tumble onto the concrete floor.

She reached out, quivering, and touched the man's hand. "Oh," she whispered, tenderly.

I climbed up behind her. "Let me help you down.

We need to call 911."

By the time I got her back on solid ground, her eyes had turned red and she was sniffling quietly.

"It's Graham Farnsworth. Our historian. Oh. I can't believe this." She was trembling as I guided her to the nearest concrete step. She sat down unsteadily, closed her eyes, and took deep, slow breaths.

My own breathing was even. I'd seen more than enough of death, both in my own experience and in my work as a police reporter. I don't find bodies or their injuries frightening, but I draw a distinction between natural death and deliberate homicide. This was no natural death.

After she dialed 911, Millicent called down to Miss Eyebrows at the front desk and ordered the museum closed. Security would be summoned to escort visitors out and, presumably, to corral them until they could take statements from everyone.

While she was on the phone, I stood by the high window and kept my gaze fixed on the parking area below, willing the police to arrive. I had seen more than enough of the body on the gallows.

Below, a tall man in an orange windbreaker appeared, heading away from the museum entrance. He broke into a trot toward the distant parking lot, where a yellow school bus was pulling in. That particular field trip was probably not going to happen.

After Millicent finished her call, I joined her on the step and we waited. I wondered whether Farnsworth had hanged himself, or if he had help, in which case a decidedly unsavory character was lurking in the museum.

"Graham Farnsworth loved the museum," Miss

Pleat said, her voice unsteady. "He served on the board of the historical society. He spent a lot of time doing research in the society library, here in the museum. He was a lovely man. I just can't believe this."

Finally, sirens signaled the arrival of police cars and an ambulance outside. I descended one level to the elevators and waited to escort the police and crime scene staff up to the turret.

They took photos and measurements before setting about the task of lowering Graham Farnsworth from the gallows. While they talked to Millicent, I called Matt Papiernik, the *Clarion*'s city editor.

"We have a situation," I said. "My feature about the Mercer Museum seems to have turned into a fatal and a police story. You'll want to alert Spencer, and let Jodi know."

I gave him the basics and hung up. Millicent had regained some of her steely composure and was making her views clear.

"I'm no psychologist, officer, but I would swear on my mother's grave that Graham Farnsworth would not take his own life."

As I waited to give my own statement, I wondered about that. A killer would have had to lift a presumably unwilling man up a ladder, wrap a thick rope around his neck, and hook him to the crossbar. It would have to be a strong killer, even if the victim were somehow incapacitated.

The detective, a plump, middle-aged man, introduced himself as Sean Parnell. I described what we saw, answered a few questions, and was given permission to depart.

I spoke briefly to Millicent Pleat, expressed my

condolences, and said we'd revisit the feature when things were more settled. I left, passing security guards at the entrance and walking through a small gathering of museum visitors who were being asked for their names and contact information. I drove straight to the *Clarion*.

Because my old door code wouldn't work, I had to check in with Destiny Rayment, who worked the front desk. Destiny always knew everything, even before just about anybody else did. She smiled and went over to the newsroom door, where she punched in the security code. "Go on back. He's there somewhere."

She knew, of course, that I'd come to see Spencer Duffy, the police reporter. Spencer saw me as soon as I entered the newsroom. He jumped up from his desk and hurried toward me with that taut, bouncy gait common to short men, as if spending a lot of time on his toes would make him seem taller.

Only a few hours had passed since the police first arrived at the museum, but Spencer had already surveyed his sources. He was perplexed, as were the police, about the scene and the appearance of the body. Spencer had agreed to withhold some of the details from his story.

"You mean they think this might be a homicide?" I asked. "I know Millicent Pleat doesn't think it was suicide."

"They're being really cagey," he said. "I think they must have seen signs of a struggle, or signs that could be interpreted that way. All we can do right now is stick to what they tell us. And, of course, what you saw."

I gave Spencer what details I could and headed out to the parking lot. After thrashing a bit and detaching my seatbelt from the windshield wiper lever on the dashboard, I buckled up and set out for home.

My hands clenched on the steering wheel. My day so far had been decidedly stressful, although I imagined that Graham Farnsworth's was worse. And Millicent Pleat's, as well. I wondered if Farnsworth had a family.

It was past noon, but I wasn't hungry. I did remember that I was low on wine, and considered that by evening, I was going to want a glass. I stopped at the state store and grabbed a basket. Despite all the complaints people make about the Pennsylvania Liquor Control Board, this store, at least, was pleasant and well-stocked. I selected an Australian cabernet and an Argentine malbec, and a frugal boxed Riesling. Near the exit, the store always stacked empty cartons for customers to take, useful for tasks such as moving. I picked up a few as I left.

When you're a loner, just about any drinking you do constitutes drinking alone. I don't care. I enjoy wine and an occasional beer, but I imbibe in moderation. Not out of guilt, but because I find the sensation of impairment decidedly unpleasant. I like to relax at the end of a rough day. I do not like to feel stupid.

Chapter Three

On Wednesday morning, I waited at my front window, and a dark red Honda Accord pulled in precisely at ten. My phone rang; it was Edmond announcing his arrival. I hurried downstairs. He stepped out of the car and extended a hand.

He was a small man, probably in his late forties, with thinning red hair and what I can only describe as a kindly face behind wire-rim sunglasses. I thanked him for his helpfulness, and we fastened our seatbelts and pulled out onto the highway.

This part of Bucks County is an endless sea of strip malls, highways, and 1950s' era housing developments, with the occasional ghost village from the eighteenth century cut off by lanes of asphalt. As we headed north, the traffic and congestion thinned out, and more leafy suburbs and fields became visible. Finally, we turned onto the river road and headed upstream.

On the New Jersey side, a similar road ran along the bank. The river was serene and smooth. A small island in mid-stream rose from a gravel beach, where two fishermen sat on folding chairs with a cooler between them and their rowboat pulled onto the shore.

"I've brought a copy of the will, which you're entitled to, but I wanted you to see the property in question. I knew your uncle fairly well, but I've only been to his house a few times," he continued. "It's a modest affair, but I do know he owned it free and clear, which should simplify things for you."

Greenwood deftly passed a dusty SUV just before the road swept around a blind curve. He slowed and drove through a small village where a row of white houses lined the road, their aged stucco exteriors showing lumps and gouges, like poorly iced birthday cakes.

The narrow road hugged the river, then crossed a humped canal bridge and followed the towpath. I thought back to my arrival in Bucks County, in the spring of the previous year.

One of my first assignments was an interview at Kingston University, which entailed crossing the river on I-95. I'd caught a glimpse of the Delaware from the bridge and marveled at the sheer profligacy of water in this region—all that water, each drop of which would be precious in Nevada, just washing out to sea!

This region was profligate, I had concluded in the intervening year. The trees produced a flamboyant crop of leaves each spring, only to toss them away in the fall. Torrents of summer rain soaked into thirsty fields, which then burgeoned in cornstalks that grew visibly taller by the day. In the fall, farmers' markets spilled over with pumpkins and squash and late tomatoes, as if the earth never grew weary of giving.

The car wound through a green tunnel, as maples and oaks met overhead and blocked the summer sun. I found my mind wandering, which I didn't like because it kept wandering back to Graham Farnsworth hanging from that gallows.

With an effort, I brought my attention back to Greenwood, who was talking about Fenton's Crossing.

"The village is so small and obscure most people have never visited it," he said, "but it was a thriving community in the eighteenth century."

The leading citizen at that time was one Eliphalet Fenton, who owned the ferry and volunteered to help Washington's forces cross the river in December 1776. Washington chose a different site, and a different ferry. Fenton, feeling slighted, decided to show them all by crossing on his own.

He set off with his ferry boat filled with comrades that frigid night, and what he did in New Jersey—or if he made it across it all—is lost to history. He refused to speak of it on his return, either from humiliation or—as he preferred to hint—because of highly secret and heroic deeds he'd performed at the Battle of Trenton.

In the next century, after an iron bridge connected the village to tiny Salter's Landing on the New Jersey side, the town grew.

We passed a produce stand with a hand-painted sign that read, "Sweet corn." Another, leaning against a wheelbarrow full of melons, said, " 'Lopes."

In 1904, Greenwood continued, a freak hurricane churned up the river, washing out dozens of bridges as it went. And from then on, Fenton's Crossing faded. The highway that once led across the bridge into New Jersey ended at the muddy banks. The new road was routed upriver to a surviving bridge, and the village essentially disappeared.

"Now, here's where you'd run into trouble if you'd tried to find the place on your own," Greenwood said. He passed a cluster of stone buildings along the road and flipped his right signal on.

He turned into a copse of trees, where a narrow

road dropped abruptly, winding down into the woods. "You'd miss this turn if you didn't know where to look."

The road crept between low hills, past blocky stone buildings, and over a tiny red-painted bridge across the canal. Just before the road ended at the river bank, Greenwood turned left into a gravel driveway that served an inn—the sign said, "Ferry Inn B&B"—and continued past several small stone cottages to where the drive widened in front of a thicket of large shrubs.

He squeezed the car through a space, hardly more than a path through the thicket, and into a small yard. A shingled structure stood before us, a square cottage with large double doors like an old garage. One of the doors had a smaller, standard-size door cut into it.

Greenwood reached for a glasses case in the console and opened it. He removed his sunglasses, folded them carefully, and exchanged them with the clear-lensed pair. He put them on and stepped out of the car. I hesitated, then followed.

"This was once a boathouse for the family that lived in the big house," he said. "In the early days, you'd use boats for transportation rather than roads, although you couldn't get far downriver because of the rapids near Morrisville until they built the canal."

He approached the small door and rummaged in his pocket for the key.

"They had it moved to higher ground after the 'fifty-five flood, using the foundation of an old carriage house that had burned down. It served no purpose after that, so they sold it off to your great-uncle.

"Anyway, it's an odd little building, and you'll find that Elias didn't do much to update it. It's still essentially two rooms, one up, one down. Let's see if this is going to open…" He jiggled the key a bit, pushed open the door and stepped in.

I followed him into a large room, smelling faintly of mothballs, and piled with cartons, files, a sagging brown couch, signs of a dingy kitchen along the far wall, and yet with a mysterious illumination from above. I looked up and saw the railing of what must be an upstairs loft, the front open to the room below. Light from upstairs windows shed a cathedral glow down upon us.

The boxes, the clutter, the old-man jackets hanging on a wooden coat rack near the door, the books and dusty journals, the scent of age, nearly made me back out apologetically, wondering how one politely refuses an inheritance. But the light streamed in parallel strips, illuminating flecks of dust our own entrance had stirred up. It caught a long spider web that stretched from the loft railing to the front wall, setting it aglow.

Maybe I'd give the house a chance.

"Now, you may want to do a bit of tidying before moving in." Greenwood was saying. He turned and spoke to me directly. "You are moving in, aren't you?"

"I've given notice on my old place," I said. "They raised the rent. I was laid off from my job. I have to go somewhere, and this is going to be it."

I'd tried to sound tough and unsentimental, but it was clear my words came out a bit pitiful, and pitiful is not my style. Greenwood looked at me sympathetically for a moment but said nothing. He walked over to the side of the room, where narrow stairs led to the loft. Paneled cupboard doors fitted into the space beneath the stairs. We squeezed past more boxes on the steps, and emerged into the upstairs room.

A rumpled brown blanket covered a narrow bed. Clothing lay draped on a worn upholstered chair; a stack of large books served as a nightstand. I quickly glanced at the title on the old, heavy volume on the top: *Conspectus Fungorum*, it read, followed by what I assumed was more Latin.

Greenwood continued chatting, as though he wanted to sell the virtues of the house. "Technically, the house belongs to the estate until it's settled, but you are free to move in any time. We left the utilities connected," he said, reaching for a light switch.

An open door toward the back revealed a toilet, and I dreaded the grunge that likely awaited. Greenwood was running down some of the particulars, mentioning things like oil heat and well water.

Dampness had left ominous patches on the sloped ceiling. I glanced out a window misted with dust. It seemed very high, looking down on a patch of shaggy grass edged with trees. Beyond the trees the river flowed slowly toward Philadelphia.

The western window, near Elias' sagging bed, looked down on the canal towpath. I knew it was unusual for the river and canal to be so close to each other, but there were places in the geography of the river valley where that was necessary, and this was one of them.

I turned to the front and leaned against the railing after carefully testing its solidity. Below was the door we'd come in. Above the door, the upstairs windows were in my line of sight. Through them I could see past the shrubbery we'd driven through into my yard. The broad driveway extended past the stone bed and breakfast to the left, and two cottages on the right, partially concealed by greenery.

Greenwood was speaking. "So, we'll have some things to sign, and I'll give you documents about taxes. I imagine you'll want to get insurance, but that's your choice, since there's no bank that has a lien on the property. A month or so after we sit down and sign everything, the county will mail you your deed.

"Oh, I should introduce you to Ruth Lovering," Greenwood said, as we picked our way down the stairs. "She lives up at the big stone house. She knew Elias well, and I took the liberty of telling her I'd be bringing you by."

Greenwood led me toward the kitchen, an array of old appliances and white-painted wooden cupboards along the back wall. The counter was covered with a jumble of coffee-making equipment and what I took to be scientific paraphernalia. We went out through a side door that led through a utility porch with a furnace, water heater and washing machine.

As we made our way back to the car, a voice said, "Edmond, I recognized thy car. May I meet my new neighbor?"

Greenwood turned and smiled as a small but erect old woman approached us through the hedge.

She had white hair pinned in a bun and wore a navy and white print blouse over a dark skirt. Her serious beige shoes had little holes punched in the leather for ventilation. She would have looked at home in an English village during the 1930s.

"I must express condolences on the loss of thine uncle, Miren. I was quite fond of him. He'd given me a key to the house to have when he traveled, just in case, although he didn't have animals or plants that needed looking after." She pressed the key into my hand

I warmed to her use of the Quaker plain speech; my father never spoke that way, but the older generation sometimes did. It seemed that Mrs. Lovering used it inconsistently, as though her habits were fading over time.

"After I heard about Elias' death, I went into the house and removed the perishables from the refrigerator. Everything else is as he left it." She offered to help in any way she could, said her goodbyes, and returned through the gap in the hedge.

We got into the Honda, and Greenwood reversed his sunglasses routine. As we drove back over the bridge and toward the main road, a large stone house came into view at the top of the hill. Ruth Lovering's, Greenwood said. It faced south, as most of the old hard-to-heat houses did. It was of exposed stone, neatly pointed, with two full stories and small dormers making a third floor. A chimney at each end emphasized its symmetry. In the mid-day sun, it glowed a warm brown against the greenery.

Greenwood was silent on the drive back. The road took us past hayfields, where the grasses crept along the road and leaned over the pavement, as though trying to escape the field through the exuberance of growth. I could hear insects buzzing, even with the windows up. Then we re-entered the green tunnel of woods, and the world changed to one of cool lushness.

Greenwood adjusted the rear-view mirror slightly. "After we'd completed the preparation of your great-uncle's will, he came by my office to sign it. He seemed anxious about something, and I was concerned he wanted to make changes. He said he wanted to get a message to you but wasn't ready to change the document itself just yet. It seems there is something about the house—or perhaps his possessions—that he very much wanted you to be aware of.

"At first, I thought it might be details about the building itself, or how to keep the furnace running. You know how conscientious people can be. But it was something more than that. He said he'd put it in a letter for me to keep in his file for you."

"Do you have it?" I was intrigued and a little apprehensive.

"No," Greenwood sighed. "He never gave it to me. He died a few weeks after that."

****

From the archives of *The Elk City Echo*:
June 19, 1974
Nuptials

Mr. and Mrs. George Laribe of Pine Camp announce the marriage of their daughter, Estelle Marie, to Richard Elias Lassiter, son of Arthur Lassiter of Whitworth, Pennsylvania, and the late Jane Lassiter, on June 10. The bridegroom is a post-doctoral fellow in the University of Nevada-Reno Department of Hydrology. After a wedding trip to San Francisco, the couple will reside in Elk City.

****

January 22, 1975
Births

To Richard and Estelle Lassiter, a daughter, January 11.

****

May 9, 1990
Community News

 Miren Lassiter, 15, daughter of Richard and Estelle Lassiter, has been named associate editor of The Marmot, *the Elk City High School student newspaper. Miren is a sophomore.*

      ****

October 16, 1990
Community News

 An essay by Miren Lassiter, a junior at Elk City High School, has been awarded first prize in the Northern Nevada English Association's essay contest. The prize brings a scholarship in the amount of $250. The title of Miren's essay is, "High School Newspapers and the First Amendment."

Chapter Four

Spencer had written a brief, careful story about the Farnsworth case. Jodi and F.X. were conferring about what, if anything, I should do with the Pleat story. In any event, it would have to wait for things to calm down so I could do a proper interview with Millicent about her years at the museum.

I took the opportunity to review my financial situation, such as it was. I sat at my desk and pulled open the flat drawer where I stashed my financial records.

Before Friday, things were quite simple. Income was comprised of my modest salary and the meager earnings from a very small trust fund. During my father's illness, he had the foresight to establish it for me, to keep it out of the unpredictable hands of my mother.

Outgo was rent, utilities, car insurance on a paid-off Corolla, internet and other tech subscriptions, groceries, wine, occasional lunches out with colleagues. I don't have expensive tastes or habits, and everything always evened out.

But now, I had severance enough to cover several weeks, and presumably unemployment for a while. Rent was no longer an issue. The main agenda item, after settling in to Fenton's Crossing, would be to look for a job.

It was time to head to Fenton's Crossing and start on the daunting process of cleaning up. And a day of scrubbing might get the image of those khaki pants off my mind's front page.

True to Edmond Greenwood's warning, I nearly missed the turn. It was hardly more than a thin spot in the greenery along the road. I managed a sharp swerve, and soon followed the lane down toward the canal and the driveway. I pulled the Corolla through the hedge and into the patch of gravel outside Uncle Elias' door. Actually, outside my door. This abode, for better or worse, was mine.

I opened the trunk and removed trash bags, rags, and a vacuum cleaner. The mop and broom were on the backseat, along with a few cartons from the state store. I set them on the gravel next to the car, fumbled with the unfamiliar lock, and pushed the door open.

I closed it behind me, sealing out the sounds of summer. The interior closed in on itself in hungry silence. My breath made an abnormally loud sound that stained the stillness, like ink on blotting paper. Light slanting into the windows picked up new swirls of dust, launched by my breathing and footsteps.

"Helloooooo!" I shouted. "Here I come, ready or not!"

The sound broke the spell, and the house was once again just a cottage where an eccentric old man had lived, a cottage in need of a good cleaning.

Uncle Elias was clearly something of a hoarder, but he was not an untidy or unclean man. The stacks of boxes were labeled, although the labels meant little to me. Files of professional papers appeared to go back fifty years. Several notebooks and folders bore logos of scientific meetings Elias had probably attended: The 1973 Conference of The American Mycological Association, Seattle. Proceedings of the European Fungus Symposium, Heidelberg, 1969.

I took a closer look at some of the vintage equipment on the kitchen counter. What I took to be an apothecary chest stood at one end, its small wooden doors labeled with spidery old handwriting that I couldn't make out. Next to it was a balance, a small oak cabinet that supported two flat, brass bowls. On the front, a metal plaque read, "Henry Troemner." A knob opened a small drawer that held an assortment of metal weights shaped like old-fashioned milk bottles. On the end of the counter stood what looked like a small, gray refrigerator, but its temperature dial suggested it was some sort of oven for heating or drying samples.

In the living room, a bank of broad, flat metal drawers with botanical labels probably held larger specimens and maps. A shelf above held several linear yards of small journal-size record books and dated ring binders, beginning in 1958. They were faded and canvas-covered until the 1970s, then covered in vinyl.

On the worn wooden desk under the window were pots of rubber cement, with drips accumulated down the sides like candle wax down a bottle of Chianti. The labels, barely readable, said, "Carolina Biological Supply Co." There was an ancient microscope, and what looked like a telescope, with various lights and mirrors that I would have to check out at some point. Everything was old, and in some cases, vintage. Elias apparently liked to stick with what he knew best.

A bulky object stood on a metal typing table. I lifted a stiff gray plastic cover to reveal an ancient manual typewriter—black iron, with "Underwood" written in gold letters. The keys were large and round. I pressed the K and the key made a satisfying crunch. I pressed the space bar and the carriage moved, smooth as silk. A flat drawer under the table held layers of white paper, thin onion skin, and a box of elderly carbon paper.

What I didn't see were photos of family or friends, travel souvenirs or mementos, awards or honors, sports paraphernalia, or trophies. Nothing suggested leisure pursuits, like books, magazines, or television.

I wondered if this was Elias' preference—maybe he was a loner, like me—or if some of the family had stopped by to collect cherished items after his death. They would have needed his will and any financial papers; maybe they took family photos as well.

A wave of indecisiveness washed over me. What should I discard? What should I preserve? What items were useful, had value, or might be interesting to another botanist? Rather than make instant decisions, I began to consolidate Elias' boxes and possessions, piling them to one side of the room for the time being.

I vigorously cleaned newly exposed floors and shelves, enough to make room for my own things on moving day. I ran the vacuum over the bare floor in the kitchen and the rather dismal tan carpet in the living room. As usual, the cord coiled around my ankle. It had clearly hoped to strangle me but had to make do with tripping.

An hour later, most of Uncle Elias' boxes and possessions were piled in a corner and atop the metal drawers, subject to review and triaging later on. The upholstered couch and chair would head for the dump on moving day, as would the bed upstairs.

I took a break and stepped out the front door. The porch, such as it was, was made of several slabs of bluestone, a gray slate that was native to the area and much used in older homes and walkways. I squatted down and pulled a few weeds from the spaces between the stones.

I suddenly sensed I wasn't alone and looked up to see a large cat staring at me. It was seated calmly about ten feet away, shaggy, and the color of a faded paper bag. It looked well-worn, as if it had had a hard life. Its muzzle had the slightly pleated look of advanced years.

"Hello, kitty," I said. It stood and padded toward me.

"Oh," said a voice behind me. "I see you've met Camel."

I turned to find a small, gray-haired woman walking toward me. She was wearing a raspberry-colored tunic over black leggings and holding a lacquered canister.

"Hi! I'm Marta Rantoul, your neighbor. Just wanted to stop by and say hello. I brought tea."

We exchanged introductions. Marta's smooth face suggested her hair was prematurely gray. "He seems friendly," I said, hesitating to pat Camel without permission.

"Oh, is he ever!" she said. "Go ahead and give him a scritch. But I have to warn you, once you've made friends with him, if you leave a door or window open, you're likely to find him on your bed."

"I'm trying to think of some sort of joke about camels' noses," I said, reaching down to rub his ears. A roaring purr erupted. "But I imagine you've heard them all before."

She smiled and nodded. "Some, but probably not all."

Marta held out the canister. "I won't stay. You try out this tea. It's a fair-trade Assam; it's subtle and fragrant, better for afternoons than for your first morning jolt. Maybe we can share a pot later when you're settled.

"Oh, and I wanted to let you know that your uncle used to share my trash bin, since we both lived alone and didn't need much space. You're welcome to continue. It's the blue one over there behind the small stone cottage." She pointed to a wheeled plastic bin next to the roadside stone cottage across the driveway from the bed and breakfast. I could see the rear bumper of a tiny red car whose front was nestled into the shrubbery.

"You can put paper out with Tuesday's trash pickup, along with the usual cans and bottles," she said. "Friday is for trash and big items like furniture."

I thanked her for tea and trash bins, and she headed back to her cottage.

I got back to my cleaning. The locksmith arrived, only a little late. He switched out the front door and kitchen door locks, recommended deadbolts for both, and handed me a bill. I wrote him a check and took possession of my shiny new keys.

My next cleaning break took me out the kitchen door to the backyard. I sniffed the summer air. The moisture itself held a scent, a welcoming, nurturing aroma so unlike the pungent air of my part of the West. I detected a particular floral fragrance, too. Sweet, a bit like honeysuckle.

Elias' property was small—no more than a quarter acre, according to the documents Greenwood had given me. It was surrounded by trees and shrubs, and the foliage almost engulfed a battered wooden shed. The leaves against the sky were clear and still, as if they were painted on blue silk.

I couldn't tell what the trees and plants were; I hadn't become familiar with Eastern varieties, and in late August, nothing had helpful blossoms to make identification easier.

Except for one small tree, in the back corner near a privet hedge. It had rough gray bark and glossy, simple leaves, and it was in full bloom. Shimmering white flowers, like small camellias, studded the branches. I inspected it more closely, and realized the flowers were the source of the sweet scent I'd noticed.

On the side of the yard, a stand of pines separated the grass from a rocky slope that led down to the river. I might trim back some of the pines to give myself a view. It would be wonderful to sit in a lawn chair in my own back yard, watching the Delaware slide past.

On the opposite side was a hedge separating my yard from the towpath. I'd keep that hedge, even if it was a bit sparse, since it provided a degree of privacy from people strolling along the towpath. As if to illustrate the point, a figure glided past, a tall young man with a metallic silver backpack. I felt protected and comfortably unobserved. I turned and looked back at the house, its dark brown shingles partially covered with vines. The kitchen window needed a good scrubbing.

Near the back porch a slab of weathered concrete, perhaps three feet across, rested on a low, circular stone wall. In the center was a large iron ring. I assumed this was a well; probably my water supply. There was a lot I needed to learn about my property.

Back in the kitchen, my phone rang. It was Jodi with an update. It had been decided that Spencer would stay with the police aspect of the Farnsworth story, but they wanted me to do the death knock—that much-dreaded interview with a recently bereaved relative. I would knock on the widow's door and ask her how it felt to hear that her husband had been discovered hanging from an antique gallows.

"Since Pleat is in limbo until she feels ready to continue, we need something for Sunday and Mrs. Farnsworth it is. I don't know if she'll be willing, but you need to try."

Chapter Five

In some ways, feature writers have it easy. We don't usually get called out in the night to witness the gory aftermath of a murder or accident or fire. We don't usually have to sit through droning hours of public meetings, hoping something reasonably newsworthy happens before deadline.

But I'd done that work earlier in my career, and I knew that—unsavory as it might seem—approaching bereaved family members is a necessary part of telling the story.

And truth be told, people usually want to talk about their loved one. In those foggy early hours and days, they often cling to the memory of the lost by telling the world about them. The public sees television reporters thrusting microphones in the faces of the bereaved and demanding a statement. In print, it's a gentler process, but an effective one.

I called Millicent Pleat to give her an update on the scheduling of her story, and to ask how she was bearing up under the difficult circumstances. It turned out Millicent knew Farnsworth's wife, Julia, and gave me her phone number.

I didn't recall Graham Farnsworth from any *Clarion* stories during my year there, so I combed the electronic morgue and added a Google search for good measure. Two stories mentioned his role as a member of the county's historic preservation board. In another, as a consultant to the re-enactment committee that oversees the annual Christmas Day crossing of the Delaware, he had argued against certain changes that he considered "ahistorical."

A young woman answered the Farnsworths' phone; she sounded too young to be Graham's widow. I identified myself and explained that I hoped the family would be willing to share their memories with the community. She listened quietly and asked me to hold for a moment while she talked to her mother.

After a long silence, Julia Farnsworth came to the phone. She sounded resigned. We had a brief conversation and settled on the next morning for an interview. If I wrote fast, I'd be able to get the story to Jodi in time for Sunday's paper.

The next morning, armed with a sense of Farnsworth's interests, and wearing one of my respectable outfits, I headed to the village outside Doylestown where the Farnsworths lived. The house was a modest one-story stucco dwelling with dark green shrubs under a picture window and two cars, a silver Prius and some kind of Volkswagen, parked in the driveway.

A young man with tousled dark hair answered the door. "Are you from the *Clarion*?" he inquired. "I'm Greg Salter, Graham's son-in-law. We're here with Mom. Come on in." He stepped aside and shut the door behind me.

In the kitchen, Greg introduced his wife, Hannah, who looked too young to be married. She had dark purple hair and an ivy-patterned tattoo emerging from a yellow T-shirt. She sat at the kitchen table with her mother.

The table held a stack of file folders, an address book, and a cell phone, along with several coffee mugs and a box of tissues. I told them I was sorry, and that I appreciated their willingness to talk about Graham during such a difficult time.

Julia, who I assumed was in her fifties, had thin brown hair and pale, watery eyes, probably due to frequent weeping. She looked like an otherwise solid and upbeat person who had sprung a slow leak and lost most of her air.

She motioned me to a chair, poured coffee into a mug, and handed it to me without asking whether I wanted it. "You were the one who found him, weren't you?" Her voice was dull, but her tone was a bit harsh, as if she was blaming me.

"Yes, I was. Millicent Pleat and I."

She asked if I intended to write about that in the story.

"I will have to mention the circumstances, but I'd like to make this story about your husband and his life," I said. "I understand he loved the museum and its library."

From there, I let her talk about Graham, his work, his interests, their family. She turned occasionally to Hannah to confirm a point. Hannah nodded from time to time but remained mostly silent.

Memories poured out. How they first met at music camp, how their friendship blossomed when they met again at Swarthmore. Graham's gentle demeanor and tenderness as a father, which concealed a driven determination to educate the world about its past. How he taught history at Hampton Friends School. How he had all the stereotypes of the rumpled, absent-minded academic. How every morning he dressed in the dark, so as not to disturb his sleeping wife, and how that courtesy sometimes resulted in fashion oddities like mismatched socks.

The Museum was his joy, she said, along with the historical society archives housed in its library. He was concerned about the loss of history, loss of old buildings and farmland, and the kinds of artifacts housed in the museum. His latest project was locating and dating all the old barns in the county, telling their stories before they either tumbled down from neglect or were bulldozed for someone's convenience. The work delighted him and kept him awake half the night with maps and old records.

I asked what she'd heard from the police about the search for his killer. I gently raised the question of suicide, which can't really be raised gently.

She looked at me steadily. "I know some are wondering if he hanged himself, and if that had been true, I would not try to deny it. But my husband was not depressed a day in his life. He didn't have the psychological makeup for it. For all his flaws, he was a happy man, eager to tackle each new interest, like the barn project.

"He would never have left this one unfinished. Not if he could help it."

I asked if funeral arrangements had been made and whether I should mention them.

"Nothing is settled yet," she said. "The police haven't released his body. That makes sense." Here her voice quavered a bit. "This was not a suicide."

She and her daughter shook their heads in unison.

"Someone did this to Graham. Someone did this to us, and he has to be found."

I used her statement to ease into a question I was obligated to ask. "Do you have any thoughts about who that might be? People who feel passionately about things, as your husband did, sometimes encounter opposition."

Julia waved her hand dismissively. "Oh, there were plenty of people who disagreed with Graham, and I suppose he could be a little intense from time to time. But nothing that would lead someone to…"

She shook her head and didn't finish the sentence.

Hannah spoke, "But Mom, didn't Dad say—?"

Julia stopped her with a look. I considered asking a probing question but decided to save the thought for later.

After we had said all that could be said, I closed my notebook and thanked her for her willingness to share her husband's life with us. I told her again how sorry I was.

She took me to the door, then turned and embraced me tightly. I'm not by nature a hugger, but I hugged her back.

Chapter Six

Moving days are always traumatic, but mine was easier than most. I'd already emptied the bookcases and packed small items away in cartons, some of which were already in the Fenton's Crossing house.

When the *Clarion* contingent arrived at my apartment around ten Saturday morning, Kevin Schmidt, the editorial page editor, was driving his red pickup. He surveyed the bedroom furniture, a computer desk, a loveseat, and bookcases, and figured they could do it all in two trips. We loaded the truck and put the remaining cartons into my car and Spencer's silver Jetta. I led the convoy to Fenton's Crossing.

I parked out in the gravel driveway, next to the other cars, so the pickup could occupy the limited space near my front door.

Mark Calabrese, the *Clarion*'s ace investigative reporter, and Ezra Blum, one of the sportswriters, wrangled my bed and box spring up the narrow stairs, while Spencer and Kevin drove back for the rest.

When the dust settled, everything was in place and I distributed pizza and cold drinks. The consensus was that I'd lucked out, abode-wise. To humble journalists, Elias' simple surroundings looked more than adequate.

The talk turned to the *Clarion*'s difficult situation. "You're lucky to be out," Ezra said, gloomily. He was a good writer and had been angling for a position in straight news. That prospect seemed less likely than ever now.

"June is pissed," Kevin said, helping himself to another slice. "She's thinking about retiring."

"Really?" I asked. "June can't retire. She's an…institution."

June Snodgrass had been the Women's Editor, back when newspapers had women's sections. Eventually, forward-looking managers had renamed the section Living, and brought in a shiny young editor to modernize things. They had assuaged the sting of her demotion by granting her a weekly column and the freedom to write whatever she wanted, immune from editing beyond matters of spelling and libel.

Poor Jodi. She clearly suffered from the burden of editing, or more accurately, not editing, June's scatterbrained prose. It had a breezy quality, like the fast-talking dialog of a 1940s movie but less coherent.

June leaped from topic to topic with no transitions and seeded her copy with archaic lingo and stereotypes that Jodi had to remove. June scanned the print edition regularly, searching for alterations to her copy. Almost weekly, she barged into F.X.'s office, bearing her column marked with angry red circles indicating unauthorized tampering.

Kevin had managed to survive the cuts, but he'd lost his assistant, which meant he had to turn out more editorials on his own or rely on syndicated copy.

"I hate that," he said bluntly. It was Kevin's job to have opinions. He offered the last slice of pepperoni around, and with no takers, helped himself.

"We're a local paper," he said, chewing." We shouldn't be using opinions from a think tank in

Chicago. Now, they're pushing me to use columns by some guy at a religious college out in Indiana. Why? Because his stuff is free."

Finally, the pizza and the chitchat dwindled. I thanked the gang warmly, and they drifted away. The sound of cars leaving dwindled away. I'd enjoyed their company, but the silence that descended on my new home felt like a healing elixir.

I arranged my meager possessions in the living room. I now had my own loveseat, along with Elias' old stained couch, which I would have to figure out how to move to the street by the following Friday. My bookcases were in place, although they were a tight fit. Elias' desk and files filled one wall, and the cupboards under the stairs took up another.

Once again, I appreciated my simple lifestyle.

I don't like to shop, and although I'm sentimental about things I've collected, I don't acquire stuff for the sake of acquiring. My wardrobe consists of my basic work uniform plus a few tailored pants and jackets that convey me to interviews or social events I might have to cover. It also included disguises: I have a small selection of garments that skew my look in whatever direction I need: Goth, proper professional, beat poet, church lady, whatever.

When necessary, I clean up good, if I do say so myself. I'm five feet nine inches with my mother's bony build and straight black hair, and light brown eyes that my father said looked like cinnamon.

And, I'm straight, by the way, not that that matters. I get tired of feeling the need to explain. Explanations sound somehow defensive. I just happen to be celibate, and my reasons are my own.

I do occasionally notice masculine pulchritude, but notice is all I do. I'm no hermit, but other than a few friends and easy relationships with colleagues, I want no entanglements. Given my natural clumsiness, entanglements are hard to avoid. I sometimes think I was put on the earth for the purpose of causing objects to tangle. Whether it's a garden hose that kinks, a vacuum cleaner cord that trips, or a scarf that strangles, any long or awkward object under my control always assumes the most inconvenient configuration possible.

But I don't seek out tangles of the human kind. All I want is my own space. I really like, and need, to balance social interactions with solitude.

It was mid-day and sunny, yet it seemed dark. The sunlight dropped heavily to the earth in a straight line, avoiding the windows. The brightness outside was blinding, but the profusion of trees filtered it so that only a greenish, underwater pallor reached into the room.

After arranging books on my shelves, I went upstairs and organized my bedroom space. I made the bed with the new sheets I'd bought as a housewarming gift to myself and put my old towels in the bathroom. Next to Elias' pile of books, which had served as his nightstand, was a wooden box, constructed with tidy dovetailing, like an extra-large recipe file.

Inside, I found photos of what I took to be Elias' travels in the western state and national forests where he conducted his collecting expeditions. Some of the photos were more recent and appeared to be taken in an office or laboratory setting, probably from Elias' Kingston University lab. In some, he appeared, with wispy white hair and a shy smile, but in most, a varied cast of rumpled scientists grinned into the camera.

At the bottom were several family photos. Some sepia toned portraits must have been of his parents and grandparents—and presumably, my own relatives. There were a few snapshots of Elias and my father next to the Range Rover he always rented on his trips, presumably taken when he'd stopped by our place to visit.

There was a color picture of my parents, evidently getting ready to go out to a social event. My father stood for Elias' camera with a boyish grin and a string tie. My mother looked prettier than I remembered, tall and dark and with a brilliant smile. She was wearing new blue jeans, freshly ironed, with a bright cotton shirt tucked in. She wore a bandana around her neck, a straw cowboy hat, and bright red lipstick. Most western women of a certain age dressed that way for casual parties—jeans and hats, but boots polished and every hair in place.

The photo was probably taken about a year before my father died and my life fell apart. After that, my mother... I don't know. I think of her as dead. I don't know whether she is or not, because she disappeared more than twenty years ago. I don't know if I miss her at all.

What I do know is that she wasn't cut out to be a wife and mother. She came from an ancient culture wherein people survived drought and oppression by...surviving. Almost every European ethnic group is a latecomer compared to the Basques, who consider themselves the ultimate survivors. Celts, Romans, assorted barbarians, Moors, fascists, they all elbowed their way into Basque territory, and none succeeded in obliterating the culture, the language, or the genes. My mother disliked being viewed as Spanish or Hispanic (or even worse, Mexican), because her family's origins were in the Pyrenees, a few meters inside the French border.

Her grandfather left Zuberoa in the 1890s and made his way to Idaho, where there was always room in the bunkhouse for another disoriented young man from the Old Country willing to be sent out alone with a summer team of horse, dog and a few hundred sheep.

Like her own mother, my mother became a cook in one of the many restaurants that catered to sheep men, and later to the broader community of diners seeking good food served family-style. And like her own mother, she charmed a young man whose labors took him out to the dry lands of the Great Basin.

My father, who taught geology at the nearly state college, came from a family of Quakers whose forebears had come to Pennsylvania on the next boat after William Penn. He was placed on earth to study it closely, and delight in the living things it nourished.

My mother was an irresistible force of nature, and my father was the trailer park. He never had a chance.

It was a stressful marriage, but my father's affection for me never faltered. He would return from a particularly grueling dispute within the department and drop his briefcase with a sigh. He would pick me up and carry me outside to watch the sunset together.

His wife, who had spent the day being irritated by that same cherub, stood clad in green silk, scented with Chanel, ready to go dancing.

She won most battles, but still she chafed. Everything in her life made her itch. Inside her tall, dark, and practical body beat the heart of a Las Vegas showgirl.

I must have dozed off on my chair, with the photo in my lap. I was awakened by a tiny scratching sound near the front door. It sounded like the skittering of a mouse, but more metallic. Wind? Branches rubbing the house? I thought I saw a shadow move on the front window curtain, but I couldn't be sure.

I crept toward the sound. It stopped. I listened for a moment, then pulled back the edge of the curtain just an inch. Nothing. For lack of evidence, I chalked the sound up to wind.

I made it an early night, checking the locks and the latches on the windows. Upstairs, I slipped between my new apple-green sheets. A pack of worries gathered just outside my conscious mind, like half-tamed animals waiting in the shadows at the edge of the clearing. What would I do about a job, and a house that was entirely my responsibility? What had Uncle Elias intended to tell me? And then there were past regrets and phobias, along with those bad years in Nevada that I had become an expert at not thinking about during daylight hours.

I did my routine: I imagined myself into an IMAX theater, settling back into a comfortable seat, and concentrating expectantly on the insides of my eyelids. The house lights dimmed, the audience quieted. Swirls and spots appeared against the darkness, undoubtedly the magnified view of capillaries and assorted debris. The swirls gradually took form, images appeared, and the show began.

****

From the archives of *The Elk City Echo*
February 5, 1992

Obituaries

Richard Elias Lassiter of Elk City died of melanoma Friday at Logan Hall Hospice in Elko. He was 50.

Born in Philadelphia, PA, Mr. Lassiter earned a degree in geology from Haverford College and a Ph.D. in geology from Harvard University. He was a professor of geology at Great Basin State College for many years.

He is survived by his mother, Margaret, of Whitworth, PA; his wife, Estelle, and his daughter, Miren, both of Elk City.

A memorial service is scheduled for 10 a.m. February 20 at Northwest Friends Meeting, Reno. Burial will be private.

Chapter Seven

Every time I wake in a new place, I have a fleeting moment of "Where am I?" panic that jolts me as much as a triple cappuccino. Instead of the familiar flat plane of my old apartment ceiling, I saw the vaulted panels, their stains dimly illuminated through dusty windows. As always, the moment passed, and I swung my feet over the side of the bed and into a pair of clogs.

In the tiny bathroom, I familiarized myself with the shower. It was rigged over a small bathtub, and the ceiling slanted down above it, leaving just enough space to stand at one end. There was rust around the faucet, but nothing that looked too dreadful. The shower curtain was ancient and blotched with mildew. I wondered if Elias kept the mold as an experiment, or maybe as a pet. I made a note to buy a fresh curtain next chance I got.

Downstairs, I boiled water on the small electric stove and made coffee. When it was ready, I took my mug to the front of the house, near the door, where I'd moved a chair. I sat and took in the cathedral effect, watching the light slant down from the upstairs east window, just miss the railing, dance with motes of dust, and stretch across the living room. I felt my spirits lift. I had hot coffee. I was in my new home. And I had it all to myself.

It's not that I dislike people, or fear them; it's that

solitude is a balm that eases stress and sharpens my thoughts. People, noise, interruptions, the unpredictability of day-to-day interactions—they all take a lot out of me.

I've worked in newsrooms my whole adult life, where tranquility and privacy are unheard of. The energized, high-pressure atmosphere brings out my abilities. I've enjoyed it, ironically enough, but my non-negotiable requirement is to retreat after deadline to my own sanctuary for recovery.

I refilled my mug and thought about the day's tasks. Unpacking and arranging, of course. And stocking up on groceries. I might grab a breakfast sandwich somewhere and then head to the supermarket and the strip mall, where I could look for a shower curtain and some new towels to go with it.

My reverie was suddenly shattered by an explosion of engine noise outside. It sounded like a jet passing way too low, or the start of a race at Bonneville salt flats.

I shot out of my chair, catching my mug as it leaped out of my hand. I checked the window by the door but saw nothing. The sound seemed to be moving around the house toward the back.

I ran through the kitchen and out the back door.

A huge man with a gray pony tail and what looked like dragon tattoos was mowing my lawn. He rode a massive red lawn tractor that looked as if it could handle a football field in no time.

Sure enough, as I stood watching him in amazement, he demolished the last patch of shaggy grass and steered the machine toward the front.

He saw me and switched off the engine. He smiled

broadly in the sudden silence.

"Good morning," I said.

"Hey, there! I didn't know you were here!" He stepped heavily off the seat and ambled toward me. "Good morning! I'm Simeon Kempe," he said, reaching a hairy hand out to shake. "I live right there." He nodded toward the small stone house nearest mine.

I introduced myself and thanked him for mowing my lawn. I wondered if this was going to be a regular thing. He answered before I could figure out a polite way to pose the question.

"After your uncle died, and the place was empty, I've been mowing every once in awhile."

"That's really nice of you," I said, and meant it. "I'll be able to do it from now on, though."

Simeon nodded toward the shed nestled against the shrubbery at the back of my yard. "I think your uncle had a push mower in there. If you can't find the padlock key, you might have to get a bolt cutter to cut through the chain. I'll lend you mine if you need it."

He turned and fixed amazing pale eyes on me.

"I'm sorry about your uncle," he said, in a gravelly voice. "He was a righteous dude. We all feel his absence."

We said goodbye, and Simeon drove his hulking machine the short distance to his shed. He stepped off to open the doors, then remounted and drove it in, crouching in the seat to clear the low door. He switched off the motor, and a lovely late summer silence descended on Fenton's Crossing.

****

The first time I'd driven back from Uncle Elias' house, I'd retraced the route along the river Edmond

Greenwood had taken. This time, after a check of the map, I tried an alternate route. It took me through woods and past cornfields in full tassel, past crossroads villages that looked unchanged from the early 1800s, over one-lane bridges, and along narrow roads where vehicles had to slow down and pull over to pass one another.

Earlier in the summer, these roadsides had been aflame with cantaloupe-colored day lilies; now the cornstalks loomed right up to the roadside, tall and green and opaque.

As I drove past, suddenly the opaque wall snapped open, revealing end-on rows of tall green separated by brown earth. Then the next second, the rows snapped back into solid green again. It made me wonder what other patterns remain obscured because we haven't seen them from quite the right angle.

My errands took less time than I expected, and as I headed back home, I made an impulsive decision to take a detour along the river to explore. I marveled at how lush and natural the banks looked. And no industry. All I saw was greenery and an occasional dock.

I found a spot to pull over, got out and stood listening to the sounds of late summer. The river was surprisingly quiet. It had been hot the last few days, and the Delaware looked tired, as though it could barely muster the energy to flow. Its level had dropped, exposing muddy brown banks. The current was brisk toward the middle, but near the bank where I stood, the water slowed and redirected itself into whirlpools and eddies.

I heard music, apparently coming from somewhere

on the river. I stepped a bit closer and found myself tangled in a honeysuckle vine growing around a shrubby cedar on the river bank. I glanced across to the Jersey side, wondering how the sound managed to carry so far. Then I heard voices. Must be boaters, I thought.

Soon the mariners came into view. Wearing hats and sunglasses and smears of white zinc oxide, they floated on large, swollen inner tubes. They had music, and attached coolers of beer, and seemed to be having a grand time as they drifted down toward the point where a van presumably awaited them. A brown snake slid through the water in S-shaped waves. I backed away and had to work to unsnare the vine from my ankle. I quickly got back into my car.

Remembering the groceries in the trunk, I headed home. By the time I unlocked the front door and carried my packages inside, it was mid-afternoon.

I put the perishables in the fridge, hoping they hadn't actually perished during my outing. Upstairs, I pulled Elias' old moldy curtain off the rod and installed my new one, a colorful turquoise and ivory stripe that I thought would go well with my new towels. I'd also bought a small oval rug in the same turquoise.

I arranged a matching soap dish and toothbrush holder on the small surface around the sink and picked up my toothbrush from the drinking glass where I'd left it.

And froze.

It wasn't my toothbrush.

Chapter Eight

It was green, like mine, and similar in style. But it clearly wasn't mine. It was even a different brand and appeared to be new. I dropped it into the sink and backed out of the bathroom.

Possible explanations rammed their way into my mind.

Someone had stayed in my house, like Goldilocks, and had left hers? I was in the wrong house? It got switched somehow while people were moving my stuff? I'd bought a new toothbrush and forgotten?

All absurd, but especially the last one. I don't forget things. I remember when I was five, camping with my parents at Spooner, or it may have been Washoe. I balked at putting on my new hiking boots because they pinched.

While my mother and I glared at each other and the boots sat near my feet, a tan shape appeared at the top of one of them. A small rattler slithered out and away into the pine needles.

It may be that my balkiness saved me from disaster. It's hard to know. But I do know that I didn't imagine that rattler.

Shortly before my father died, we went through a box of old vacation photographs, the color starting to fade after ten years. And there I was, sitting on a log, wearing the boots, glaring into the camera. My mother had bought them impulsively, as she did so many things. Who buys expensive footwear for a growing child?

When I saw the picture, I remembered and described my memory to my father. He confirmed every detail, from the boots, which apparently had caused some discussion between him and my mother, to the snake, to taking the picture of me on the log.

If I remember something, it happened. If I don't remember it with a bit of prompting, like an old photo, it didn't happen. No false memories, no hallucinations.

Someone had been in my house, in my bathroom, since this morning, when I knew I had used the correct toothbrush.

I rummaged under the bathroom sink for a plastic bag and wrapped the mystery toothbrush in it, then sat on the bed to think about what to do next.

Should I call the police to report a burglary? Of a toothbrush?

Think about who might have keys to the house?

Move out and find somewhere else to live?

Pack an overnight bag and head for a hotel right now?

And then there was the question of why. Why would anyone break into a house and switch toothbrushes? Why take only that?

Or did they take only that? I glanced nervously around the room, looking for signs of disruption. Nothing looked different, but I couldn't imagine anything worth stealing concealed among my humble belongings anyway.

I went downstairs and did a complete survey of the first floor, double checking my new, freshly changed locks as I went. They were properly secured, and I couldn't see any signs of damage. Nothing was out of place. Elias' boxes and scientific instruments were where I had left them. I pulled open the specimen drawer and the map drawer. Nothing looked disturbed.

I decided to do nothing. It seemed pointless to call the police to report a missing toothbrush, and I suspected I'd be viewed as delusional.

Which I was not.

Chapter Nine

It was late summer. I'd been settled into my new home for nearly a week, and during that time, it hadn't rained. The river was looking worn; dry islets emerged in the river bed. It looked as if I could walk across the dry parts and ford the rest, but I would never actually try, because the currents were deceptive. Every summer the *Clarion* published tragic stories of people drowning in the Delaware.

I was getting acquainted with the river, the canal, the towpath, and the walkers and joggers, and occasional horse I saw there. I enjoyed my morning coffee and evening wine seated in a lawn chair in my backyard, where I'd lopped a few branches from the white pine to gain a view of the river.

At dusk, bats swooped noiselessly through the deepening shadows, and after darkness had fallen completely, the nocturnal symphony began. It opened with low, rhythmic grunts, presumably from baritone frogs, then added the higher, soprano peeping of tree frogs. And layered above was the chorus of crickets, and some kind of night bird that keened to its own beat.

I was of two minds about inviting Marta over for tea. For a while, I considered keeping her at arm's length, in the interests of privacy. But she'd given me the tea, and she'd offered to share her trash bins with me. So I'd left a note on her door, and the next afternoon, she showed up at mine, full of cheer.

I had steeped the loose tea in my metal coffee pot and hoped for the best. I had milk and sugar, but no little cookies. This was not going to be particularly English, although I was using my best tea service: two mugs, one emblazoned with Elk City Rocks and the other with Harrah's.

I brought a tray to the coffee table and poured a mug for Marta. She skipped the milk but stirred sugar into hers. Despite my preference for black coffee, I like my tea loaded, English style.

There was something hungry in her green eyes as they darted around my house. Clearly she was assessing my space, if not actually judging it. She was wearing another textured tunic, this time in a rich aquamarine linen.

I told her about my former job, and my current freelance efforts. Marta said she was a fiber artist, converting wool and sometimes silk into woven or felted hangings and other decorative textiles.

It was enjoyable listening to her describe her projects as I sipped my tea, a luxury for a reporter for whom interesting stories are usually accompanied by the furious scribbling of notes.

I reassessed Marta's age downward. She didn't look much older than me, although the silver hair was misleading. I wondered idly why she didn't color it. People probably wondered idly about my minimalist approach to fashion, too.

She set down her mug and looked around appraisingly.

"So, are you going to fix the place up?"

Then, perhaps sensing that her words might seem

abrupt, if not critical, she added, "I mean, make it more your own?"

I wasn't offended. Décor is not a point of pride with me, and I said so. "It is kind of Geezer Chic at this point. But it suits me. Really, I'd never thought much about the house from an aesthetic standpoint."

It was true. For me, a dwelling was a place to sleep and a place to retreat, a private sanctuary. I'd never given much thought to how it looked.

"It's not a matter of being vain or extravagant, you know," she said. "The space you live in matters. It affects how you feel, how well you work. And this is your workspace.

"You don't need a decorator; no," she added, "that's not you at all. You need a neighbor who can throw together a sketch or two."

My shoulders tensed a bit. Marta was being generous, but I didn't need someone bounding in and out of my space, waving tape measures and fabric samples around.

I offered her more tea, then stood and turned the heat on under the kettle. Marta sprang from the love seat and asked, "May I use your bathroom? Tea does this to me."

I motioned to the stairs, and off she went. I hoped the bathroom was tidy enough; I hadn't anticipated her needing it when her own was so near. But tea does that to a person.

The toilet flushed upstairs. I waited for Marta to return.

The bathroom door opened, then closed. At least a minute passed before I heard her feet on the stairs.

Chapter Ten

There were those damn tan pants again. I shuddered inwardly. These, however, extended from the kneehole of my computer desk. I watched as Pradip wrangled a snarl of cables and cords from an assortment of equipment into the appropriate plugs and sockets.

I marveled at his skills. Not only did he solve the *Clarion*'s IT and tech problems, seemingly without effort, he also had a certain grace when it came to the physical world that eluded me.

Despite my need to keep people at arm's length, there was something about Pradip that put me at ease. He never pried. He chatted openly about his own life, but was always satisfied with whatever details, if any, I supplied about my own. I leaned against the wide file cabinet and watched him finish up.

After one last burst from the electric drill, Pradip backed out, stuffed a few coils under the desk, and stood up.

"I put a power strip under there, so your wires won't be as tangled. Here's the master switch." He flipped a red toggle. "I have both your desk unit and laptop hooked up to your printer, so you're good to go. You're not getting a landline, are you?"

I shook my head. I'd arranged for cable and internet but planned to rely on my cell phone. "I can't thank you enough. You did all of this so fast. I never would have figured it out on my own."

"No problema." Pradip smiled as he tossed spools of wire into his satchel. "Regarding my fee, how about we scratch the pizza and check out that pub down on the highway? Treat me to a brew and we'll call it even."

We took both cars and within minutes turned into the Star and Garter parking lot. I realized we could have walked. The pub was probably no more than a quarter mile away.

We entered and eight heads turned our way. The hum of conversation ceased, then resumed. Three men sat at the bar, wearing work clothes and feed caps. Behind the dark wooden bar, brilliant bottles and glassware gleamed like jewels on shelves in front of the mirrored wall. Two other men seated at a table were younger, and wore oxford cloth shirts, khakis, and loafers. A pair of older, academic-looking men occupied another table. One handed some kind of diagram to the other, who took off his glasses and held the paper at arms' length.

Pradip picked a table as I stepped to the bar to order. I read the labels on the pump handles and ordered a Guinness and a Harp.

The bartender had a neatly trimmed gray beard and a distinct Irish accent. He filled the glasses and let them sit while the foam settled.

"Sit yourself down, lass. I'll bring these to your table."

I thanked him and joined Pradip.

Keeping his voice down, he said, "Okay, I can't put my finger on the zeitgeist here. Sports? Biker? Gay? Clearly not standard pickup." He nodded sideways toward the other patrons.

"You're way off the mark," I whispered. "Biker, no way. Probably not sports, although there is a TV. Gay? Hard to tell."

We both listened to the hum of conversation. I heard one of the young men in business casual at the next table say something about "taking ownership" and "strategy actualization."

The bartender brought the foaming glasses to the table and guessed correctly that the Guinness was for Pradip. "I'm Desmond Sweetman, proprietor, at your service," he said.

We introduced ourselves.

"I just moved to Fenton's Crossing," I said. "Pradip's been helping me set up my computer. Are you by chance from Ireland?"

"I am," Desmond said. "I came to this part of Bucks twenty years ago and was horrified to learn that there wasn't a proper pub within miles. I had to open one myself, then, didn't I?"

"But there are lots of them down in the lower part of the county," Pradip said. "Bensalem, Levittown— there are Irish pubs everywhere."

"Ah, but I said proper, now, didn't I? I've been in some of those places. They put a neon shamrock in the window and serve green beer on St. Patrick's Day, if you can imagine that." Desmond shuddered. "As it happened, this place came available. It was sadly abandoned, having been a school house long ago."

I looked over at the bar and the paneling on the wall behind the mirrored shelves. "It looks as though it's always been here."

"And I thank you for that! Ah well, welcome to the

Crossing, Miren. Hope the natives are making you welcome."

He turned and went back to his post.

The door burst open, and a burly middle-aged man walked in and took a stool at the bar. The men with diagrams glanced up from their work and looked at him intently.

Pradip settled in with his Guinness and filled me in on *Clarion* developments. "No more layoffs, but Frank Killian gave notice yesterday. They cut his pay, starting next cycle. He told them he'll work at his old rate until then, and then he walks. I have no idea what he plans to do after that."

The newcomer sat with his back tense, swiveling back and forth on the stool. As he did, he noticed the men with the blueprints, and stood. I couldn't hear their conversation as he approached their table, but the body language of all three men suggested a rocky relationship.

Finally, the man standing said loudly, "You want to take that back?" Desmond moved down the bar to monitor the situation.

The men at the table said something I took to be conciliatory, but the other man spun on his heel and stormed out the door. I wondered if he had paid.

We all watched the door swing shut, then returned to our routines.

"I wouldn't be surprised if you get a call," Pradip said. "F.X. is showing signs of stress. He's desperate for bodies to cover meetings."

"Well, what did he expect?" I took a big gulp of Harp and tried to suppress a burp. That took chutzpah, I thought. Lay off your staff and then complain you're understaffed. Although I realized that F.X. wasn't the decider in these matters.

"How about you? I assume you're in a good situation, right?"

Pradip nodded and explained the intricacies of information technology, the lifeblood of the modern newspaper. The *Clarion* would be rudderless without him.

As would I. I thanked him again for his work. "I really appreciate this, Prad. You're going to make some tech-illiterate girl very happy someday."

"I suspect that project is being worked on even as we speak." He turned his glass thoughtfully, eyeing the rings of foam that marked each sip on the inside of the glass. "My aunt is very good at this sort of thing, and I'm sure she's sending hot tips to my parents regularly."

"And that doesn't bother you?" I tried to imagine the horrific potential of having my semi-dysfunctional family arrange matrimony for me.

"Not really. I'm allowed considerable input into the process. It's no worse than having your Mom nudge you about getting married and setting you up with blind dates. I'm afraid you're not going to make the cut, though, at least in the first round. They're not big on Basques in West Bengal."

We chuckled and clicked glasses. I went to the bar to settle the bill, and Desmond beamed at me. "Don't think of it! This is with my compliments. You'll be back."

****

I'm no Luddite, but I dislike those aspects of technology that interfere with my privacy and independence. A cell phone is a necessity, but social networking is not. I'm happy to have my past and lost youth remain past, and lost. I dread the idea of people popping up out of the blue, needing to be either friended or not, perhaps becoming resentful if I don't respond.

One exception is blogs, on a few of which I hang out as a regular, if anonymous contributor to the comments that follow each post. My favorite, *WonkLikeMe*, focuses on books, writing and political humor. Its commenters form a pseudonymous, yet oddly intimate, community.

Pradip had done well. After a few stumbles, I found my way through the various log-ons and sign-ins and clicked on the blog. McGonif, the blogger, had posted a snarky comment about something foolish the Senate Minority Leader had said. The post was followed by comments, which immediately departed from the topic at hand and veered into weather, dog training difficulties, vegetable harvests, personal health crises, and links to amusing YouTube videos.

I'd come to the blog several years ago, following links from various alarming news stories, and found that many of the commenters were journalists. The conversation veered toward the perils of that industry as much as anything else, and it was enjoyable hanging with people who wrote well and cheerfully pounced on any and every spelling or grammatical error their commenting friends made. McGonif was notorious for lazy typing, so we all took delight in correcting and shaming him.

I entered the fray.

Basquette Case: Greetings, all. I'm moved in! Just had my own Nerd R Us out to hook me up.

Flora: Yay!

Rapscallion: Congratulations on your new place, B.C. Were you pleasantly surprised?

Basquette Case: Um, definitely surprised, Rap. Small, jammed with junk. I'm just starting to clear out.

Flora: Any job prospects?

Basquette Case: That's going to have to wait. I can manage for a while, since I'm not paying rent, and I have a few freelance projects. But yeah, I'll have to get serious once I'm settled. So, how's by you? Is your cat dealing with the newbie?

Flora described the trials of introducing her new rescue cat to her seventeen-year-old Maine Coon. She was also busy canning and regaled us with her struggles with jars and lids and huge pots of boiling water.

Flora: I'm almost done. The jars are on the counter, and I'm waiting for the lids to seal.

Rapscallion: Achooo!

Basquette Case: Allergies bad this year, Rap?

Rapscallion: The worst. If we have a dry summer, they say that's what makes the pollen worse. They say the same thing if we have a wet summer.

Flora: *pop!*

Mrs. Calabash: Greetings, all.

Rapscallion: Hey, Mrs. C. Did that tornado miss you yesterday?

Mrs. Calabash: Missed us, but not the next town over. Serious damage. Everybody's okay, or so we're told.

Flora: *pop!* *pop! pop!*

Basquette Case: That must be very satisfying, Flora.

Flora: Oh, it is! Means everything worked out.

Hey, Hodge, get away from that...hot! hot!... Must away before I have cats in the water bath.

I marvel at the way simple text on a screen conveys so much about another's temperament, intellectual wattage, and levels of compassion. I had never seen any of my fellow commenters in the flesh, and in quite a few cases didn't know their age or gender.

Yet I can easily pick out which are warm-hearted, which are cold; which are fussy and sensitive; which have encyclopedic knowledge and which have the intellectual nimbleness which is a different thing entirely. Some pout when ignored; others can't resist the urge to one-up everyone else. I can even sense when someone's had a few too many.

I bade farewell and logged off. Time to clear out some of Uncle Elias' files and boxes.

I'd almost forgotten the wide metal cabinet under the boxes I'd stacked above and in front of it. I shoved the cartons to the side and saw that it had six large, flat drawers, designed for maps or prints. I slid the top one out and beheld an array of desiccated pine needles, glued to what looked like thick laboratory blotting paper. Number codes of some sort had been written on the corner of each sheet.

The next four drawers contained more of the same. The bottom one opened roughly but yielded what to me is treasure: maps! There were dozens, some yellow and torn. The ones visible on the surface appeared to be the seven-minute U.S. Geological Survey maps used by hikers and people who work outdoors, as my father had done. Apparently Uncle Elias used them on his collecting expeditions.

I love maps in the same way that I love floor plans;

I find it satisfying to look down on terrain or a building from above. I love the way an aerial view reveals things that might be obscured at ground level, whether it's a tiny lake hidden between hills, or a cleverly concealed closet tucked behind a wall.

I carefully lifted the top layer out and set them on the coffee table. Some were covered in red dots made with a colored pencil, presumably showing the range of…something.

It was clear that these were Rocky Mountain and Great Basin maps; I shuffled through them until I found several that showed terrain I was familiar with. I squinted at one showing an area in Pershing County that I knew well.

Too well.

I felt a familiar chill rise from my feet to my heart. I slid the map to the bottom of the stack and replaced them all in the drawer. It made a cold metallic sound when I closed it.

Chapter Eleven

The next day's mail included a hand-delivered note from Marta. I dropped the mail on the counter and opened the envelope. It was on heavy, textured card stock, probably handmade.

I'm weaving all afternoon. If you'd like, drop by and see my space. Use the side door.

~M.

I hesitated for a moment, but finally picked up my key, locked the door behind me, and walked past Simeon's cottage to Marta's side porch. I stopped to look at the roughly laid red shale wall. In afternoon sunlight, the reddish-brown color looked alive somehow, as though life-giving blood coursed through its veins.

I heard a thumping sound that stopped as soon as I knocked. In a few moments, Marta opened the door and smiled in welcome.

She led me through a small kitchen with wooden cabinets painted a butter yellow, into what had been the cottage's living room but was now Marta's studio. A huge wooden loom filled the far side of the room, capturing sunlight that streamed in through southern windows. Against another wall was an old draftsman's table. A narrow ledge behind the tilted surface held cups for brushes and bowls with tubes of acrylic paint. Clearly, this was where she painted out her designs before creating the textiles.

"I'm working with undyed wool from the sheep just up the towpath,' she said, showing me thick skeins of wool. "They're Shetlands, a heritage breed with unbelievably soft wool. I have three colors, as you can see—ivory, chocolate and black."

To one side was a spinning wheel and smaller tools of the weavers' trade. She showed me bobbins, spiky carders, and wooden objects shaped like giant jacks that she called "kniddie knoddies," for winding yarn into a skein.

I recognized quite a few of the tools from the Mercer Museum, then shuddered inwardly at the other memories the museum held for me.

She told me how she selects the fleeces at the farm, then meditates on them—stroking, tugging at them to sense the crinkle, touching the wool to her cheek to ascertain its ultimate softness.

"Come on, I'll show you some of my felt work," Marta said. I followed her into a small den, where she had a desk with a clunky old computer, and a dark green recliner next to a table stacked with books. Camel the cat snoozed on the chair, curled like a cinnamon bun. Large abstracts in dark reds and blues hung on two walls; on closer inspection I saw that they were constructed of layers of felt, in an appliqué style.

The desk and shelves held found objects—pine cones, rocks, shells, a feather from what I guessed was an eagle. Among these she included thick candles, an antique clock, and a stoneware crock filled with paintbrushes.

"They say certain visual arrangements reduce stress," she said as we walked into the kitchen, where the yellow cabinets and cream-colored walls brightened the north-facing room. "But you can go too far. Too much symmetry feels flat, so you have to include small surprises."

She turned on the heat under the kettle. "I don't know if reducing stress is always the best way to get going on an art project, but I know that when I go into the studio and feel the light and colors wash over me, I am ready to make something beautiful."

She turned and leaned against the stove. "Now, I'm a visual person. I work with the visible world. Your work is different, but it's still creative. When I talk about your space, I'm thinking about how you might arrange it to enhance your work."

It was nice that Marta saw me as an artist, but I didn't agree. Reporters have been cranking out copy in the most grimy and gloomy of spaces for centuries. It's almost a point of pride that we aren't fussy about having neat files or pretty bouquets in our desks.

But I liked what I saw, and it occurred to me that Elias' house—my house—would profit from some visual improvements. It had potential.

I asked Marta if I could take another look at her weaving project. She seemed pleased with my interest and set about putting sugar and cups on the table.

Back in the large studio, I examined the textile that was accumulating at the lower end of the loom. Using her three natural colors, Marta had created a series of waves that washed across the blanket or hanging she was working on. The pattern was abstract, but the traditional materials made it seem grounded and real.

One of the studio's windows faced our shared driveway and the Ferry Inn. In the small yard behind the stone building, a young woman was working among the plants in one of several raised beds. She put something green into a bag slung across her shoulder, and when she turned her back, I saw she also carried a baby in a purple mesh carrier that allowed pink legs to swing freely.

On the way back to the kitchen, I glanced out the study window and saw that Marta had a better view of the towpath than I did; she could see quite a distance in both directions from her window. I wondered where the bathroom was. I briefly considered asking to use it, and checking on Marta's toothbrush inventory. Instead, I returned to the kitchen.

Marta poured tea into heavy mugs that showed the slight imperfections of the hand crafter's work. She gave me a brief history of the cottage and its former owners. She told how her own art of hand weaving was resurrected by craftsmen in the small riverside town of New Hope in the 1920s, along with other Arts and Crafts specialties.

"I like your cottage very much," I said. "It doesn't look decorated; rather, it looks inviting."

"See? Inviting. That's what you want a workspace to do—invite you in, not chase you out. If you'd let me come over and do a quick measure, I could jot down a few ideas—furniture arrangements, possible color schemes. You could do as much or as little as you like."

I produced what I hoped was a noncommittal nod, then changed the subject. "What can you tell me about the other Fenton's Crossing residents? I met Simeon a few days ago, but that's about it."

"Oh, Simeon!" Marta laughed, but didn't elaborate. I wasn't the only one changing the subject, because

Marta moved right along. "Right here," she said, waving her hand to indicate our shared driveway area, "there's Simeon, you, me, and the Butterfields, who own the bed and breakfast. Paul and Melanie. And, of course, Ruth Lovering in the big stone house, plus a few more along the road."

Marta set her mug down firmly and fell silent. I concluded that the discourse on neighbors was over. I finished the last bit of tea and stood up, thanking Marta for the tea and studio tour.

The gravel crunched under my feet. I stepped through the hedge, wondering if Marta was going to be a problem. The idea of a very observant person sizing up my space, my stuff, my taste in bath mats, gave me pause.

Once inside, I surveyed my domain. Discolored white walls, except where the original worn wood paneling remained from the boathouse days. Unpainted window sills, gray-tan carpet in the living room. Nothing on the walls. Definitely dismal, yet I did my work here and had no need for particular colors or decorations or amulets to crank out a good story.

Then I recalled my own impression when I first saw Elias' house with Edmond Greenwood, and was moved by the light stretching down from the upstairs windows. Maybe Marta had a point.

I turned and realized I hadn't really inspected the cabinets under the stairs closely. The shorter one, near the lower steps, contained small gardening items. Under an unglazed flower pot in the back, I found a chrome key.

I remembered the shed out back, which I had ignored since Simeon pointed it out to me on the morning he mowed my lawn.

I took the key and went out the back door to the padlocked shed door. The key fit but resisted my efforts to turn it in the lock.

Finally, reluctantly, the hasp fell open. I opened the door, which squeaked on rusty hinges. Inside was a push lawn mower, covered with cobwebs and dust, but fairly shiny and evidently well maintained. I was pleased to see it, because the lawn was a bit shaggy and I would just as soon do it myself than have Simeon be his helpful self again.

The tiny shed held a few shovels, a leaf rake and a long-handled pruner. Behind everything was a wooden ladder, slanted to fit beneath the low roof. That appeared to be all. I decided to add the few tools and pots I was salvaging from the cupboard and continue to keep it locked. There was no pressing reason, except to deter anyone with designs on my property.

Back inside the house, I wondered what ideas Marta would have for my house. Sure, a little paint would help, but it was an old structure with one big room, a kitchen along the back wall, and stairs to one side. Aesthetics could only do so much.

If I squinted, and used my imagination, I could clear out the clutter, throw some paint on the walls, hang some prints, and spruce up the lighting. Only a week in and the place was growing on me.

Chapter Twelve

Soon after Labor Day, summer ended abruptly but deceptively. The days remained hot and dry, even dusty. But every evening I was surprised by the sudden fall of darkness that drew me indoors. Tonight, a cool rain drained the remaining warmth from the earth, and suddenly I found myself grateful I'd figured out the heating system and thought to order an oil delivery.

The rain turned torrential; then, around seven p.m., a flash lit the living room, followed by a loud crack. All the lights went out.

I unplugged my laptop and sat in the gloom. Did I have candles? What would work without power? Heat? Probably not. Plumbing? Probably not, since the pump on the well would be useless. I was pretty much helpless until the power came back on.

And yet, it wasn't entirely unpleasant. Silence descended. I allowed my thoughts to wander.

A light knock on the front door startled me awake. The rain had stopped. I stumbled through the darkened room and peeked between the curtain and the side of the front window. The hood of a pink plastic anorak came barely above the door handle, and a small hand reached up and knocked again.

I opened the door. The child was holding two flashlights and handed one to me. "We're going to Mrs. Lovering's. Everybody does when the 'lectricity goes out." She turned and ran away, her progress across the footbridge and up the hill marked by splashes of light from her own torch.

So who was that? And why did everyone go to Mrs. Lovering's in these circumstances? Did she have some kind of generator? Might as well put on boots and windbreaker and head on over, and perhaps all would be made clear.

Before locking up, I put a bottle of Merlot *ordinaire* in a tote bag, just in case. Carrying the tote and the flashlight, I picked my way up the slope.

The door of Ruth Lovering's house was made of oak planks, hinged with wrought iron bands. I lifted the heavy ring in the center, and let it drop with a surprisingly loud clunk. The door creaked open, and its owner stood in the light from a huge fire crackling on a massive hearth.

"Miren? Do come in. Give me thy coat, and pull this chair up to the hearth."

Six or seven people hitched chairs and benches to make room for me in the circle of soft light. The stone fireplace occupied most of the wall and was tall enough to sit inside. A log roared on an iron grate. The girl who had knocked at my door sat on a three-legged stool near the flames.

"Nice welcome, isn't it?" said a man to my left. It took me a moment, but I recognized him as the man who had barged into the Star and Garter a week ago. He had the look of a man who had once been very strong, and who retained some of that strength in his middle years despite some extra pounds. The worn T-shirt that stretched across his belly beneath an unzipped sweatshirt said, as far as I could see, "Middletown

76

Grange Fair."

"Suppose you expected electricity and all sorts of modern conveniences in Fenton's Crossing," he said, grinning.

A slim woman I took to be his wife sat next to him, a tentative smile playing over a thin and anxious face. To her other side was Marta.

"Does this happen a lot around here?" I asked him. He nodded ruefully, and Marta spoke up.

"Unfortunately, yes. We used to just drive somewhere that had lights and wait it out. But nothing compares with Ruth's place."

Ruth approached the fire carrying a black Dutch oven with a long, looped handle. Using a potholder, she swung a long hook from the side wall of the fireplace and hung the pot over the fire.

She straightened and proceeded to make introductions, beginning with the man in the T-shirt.

"This is Jim Bollinger and his wife, Ellen, who live down on the highway, and Marta Rantoul, who's in the cottage at the end of the driveway." Marta smiled, and we nodded.

"On the hearth here is Tina Butterfield, who belongs to Paul and Melanie. They own the bed and breakfast." Melanie was holding a sleeping baby, whom Ruth introduced as Nell.

Melanie had a sweet, pink-cheeked face and big brown eyes that, despite her youth, looked tired. Paul, an earnest looking man with a dark moustache, nodded in welcome.

"And this is Simeon Kempe, in the cottage between you and Marta," Ruth said, and we nodded like old pals. Next was Roberta Jennings, a lean black woman who appeared to be in her sixties. She smiled and said, "I'm in the stone house across from the Bollingers, right next to the pub on the highway."

Ruth turned and moved toward a door to what I assumed was the kitchen, and Roberta stood to follow her.

I began to get up. "Let me help you!" I called after her.

"Thee'd help best by sitting, Miren. I know my kitchen, and at my age, I do best by following my old habits."

Presumably Roberta was familiar with Ruth's old habits. They returned a few minutes later with a tray laden with bowls, spoons, and napkins. Roberta held the tray while Ruth ladled stew out of the iron pot.

Paul took drink orders, and I handed him my bottle. He headed into the kitchen as Ruth distributed bowls of exquisitely savory stew.

As the conversation drifted toward village chit-chat, I found myself balancing my stew and wineglass, and glancing around the large room. Much of it was in flickering shadow, but other areas were warmly lit by oil lamps. Two heavy doors faced one another across the wide plank floor—the one I'd come in, and a back door directly opposite.

A small cupboard was set into the wall next to the back door. Deep window sills indicated the thickness of the stone walls.

Jim Bollinger had left his chair and was wandering around the room, checking his phone. I imagined the original residents of the house marveling at what technology had wrought over the centuries.

Roberta Jennings turned her gaze on me. Her dark

eyes gleamed behind rimless glasses.

"Miren Lassiter. I've seen that name recently. You wrote the article about Graham Farnsworth in the *Clarion*, didn't you?"

I said I had. Roberta nodded. "You captured him well. I've known Graham for years. We shared an interest in local history. Poor Julia. What a shock that must have been. He never seemed like the type to have enemies."

So Roberta attributed Farnsworth's death to malice. Yet Spencer's article had not mentioned the authorities' suspicions.

She looked thoughtful. "But when you think about it, he did cross people over the years."

Roberta seemed to cast a glance at someone else in the room, but I couldn't tell who. I considered pursuing this line of conversation, but Roberta had shifted the topic back to history.

"This house is clearly dates from—what was it, Ruth?—1762? There may have been a dwelling even before that, but that likely would have been a log house.

"Now, the smaller structures nearby may have housed people who worked on the land—Marta's and Simeon's cottages, for example. Of course, yours was an early boathouse.

"The houses along the road, like mine and Jim and Ellen's, were most likely the houses of tradesmen. The early census records describe tanners, blacksmiths, wheelwrights and the like."

Someone asked Melanie and Paul about their guests, and were assured that fortunately they were guestless tonight. They were pondering investing in a generator for just this sort of eventuality, however.

The room was silent for a while, as everyone seemed content with their own thoughts and the sounds of the hissing logs. The fire cast unpredictable shadows on our faces, as fires have done since people began to gather around them.

Suddenly, light filled the room. There was a clunking sound from the basement, and the whir of a refrigerator coming back to life in the kitchen. The power was back.

The spell was broken. We carried our bowls into the kitchen and moved our chairs back against the wall. As we collected our coats and flashlights, I, in my turn, thanked Ruth for her hospitality. At the door, she replied in a whisper, "I'm almost sorry when the power comes back on."

I picked my way down Ruth's flagstone path, past her round stone well with its heavy timber lid. The sound of water inside made a bell-like echo from deep within the ground. I thought about wells and their essential role in these old homesteads. Something about the distant sound made me think about peril, as well; the danger of children falling in, the danger of earth caving in on the well diggers. Like fire, a presence for good or ill.

****

The next afternoon, I stopped at the B&B to return the flashlight. Tina met me at the door and let me into a small, dim rustic parlor. In one corner, a wooden bar remained, complete with a lattice structure suspended above with wrought iron hardware. This structure, I remembered reading, would be lowered at closing time to keep thirsty guests away from the ale.

The Butterfields had incorporated it into the room's

arrangement, placing an inviting settee in front where patrons would have stood. On the surface, along with pewter pitchers and stoneware crocks, a rack of brochures advertised local sightseeing opportunities.

The room seemed full of doors. One was closed; in the corner, a door stood open, revealing the wedge-shaped steps of a winding staircase. Another open door must lead to the kitchen, where I could hear voices.

Melanie was saying, "Are you going to finish up the holes in the floor so I can move that thing back?"

There was an inaudible man's response.

I handed Tina the flashlight with my thanks.

"What's the rest of your name?" she asked.

"My whole name? It's Miren Lassiter."

"No, I mean Miren. Is it part of a bigger name?"

"No, just Miren. Is Tina part of a bigger name?"

Tina nodded. "It's Sestina. That's a kind of poem. It's a hard poem, and my dad said he was ground and determined to write one. And he did! He liked it so much he named me after it."

"Ah. He must have liked it really a lot."

Melanie came into the room, carrying a wicker laundry basket and the baby. "Oh, hi, Miren. I assume you got your power back too?"

"I did, thanks. Can I take that for you?"

I'd meant the basket, but Melanie held the baby out. "It would be better if you could hold Nell for a minute while I throw these in the machine."

I hoped I didn't flinch too obviously. "I'm actually not very good with babies," I said, "even cute ones like Nell." The baby gazed at me with big brown eyes above rosy cheeks.

I was rescued by Paul, who at that moment walked

in from the kitchen. He grabbed the baby and gave her a bounce. "There's a lot of that cobbler left, Mel. Think it will keep till tomorrow? Hi, Miren."

"It'll be fine. I might serve it with tea when they get back from Ringing Rocks this afternoon," Melanie said, opening the door that must lead to the basement. She turned and said, "We have new guests—a couple who arrived this morning. Pretty good timing." She hustled down the stairs.

I opened the front door to let myself out. "I just stopped over to return your flashlight," I said to Paul. "I enjoyed the gathering, even if it's inconvenient to be without power."

"The past is a great place to visit," Paul said, "but I wouldn't want to live there. Stop by again."

As I left, I thought he actually did live there. The house looked like…what? Currier and Ives? With snow, it would definitely look like a Christmas card, or one of those paintings famous for shimmering with light.

My next stop was Mrs. Lovering's. I did not intend to tell Mrs. L. about the toothbrush. But I could ask, in a roundabout way, how someone might get in. Maybe it wasn't a matter of locks; maybe someone knew a loose board somewhere that allowed access. Whatever, Ruth would be the one to know.

I crunched across the gravel drive, across the footbridge, and onto the gray slate path that led to Ruth Lovering's door.

Accompanied by the aroma of cinnamon, Ruth answered in a dark skirt, a neat tan blouse, and a white cardigan. She wore a mitten-shaped pot holder on her right hand and smiled in welcome. She turned and we stepped inside. This was the same large room I'd spent time in last night, but it looked entirely different in daylight.

We stepped onto broad pine boards, originally rough cut but smooth with age and footsteps. I settled in a carved chair with velvet upholstery and gazed across the room at the massive fireplace I'd sat in front of last night. The remains of a charred log lay on the grate. I could see the heavy wood lintel above the fireplace; a pattern of chinks in the wood showed where the board had been shaped with an adze. Pewter and silver plates stood upright on the narrow mantel.

Ruth checked her oven, then came back and sat on the couch near me. I thanked her again for her hospitality, then said, "I have a feeling someone has been trying to get into my house, maybe successfully. I felt I had to ask you about Elias' key, and who might have had access to it."

Ruth looked concerned, then gazed at the floor as she tried to recollect. "Oh, dear. Let's see. I've had that key for years, and I'm sure it was in its place in the chest of drawers until the day I gave it to thee, shortly after you'd moved in. I can't imagine anyone stumbling across it, or knowing what it opened, since it wasn't labeled. But it is worrying. You have had your locks changed, haven't you?"

I nodded. "Do you know if there's some way into the house I might not have thought of?"

She shook her head slowly. "Thy house isn't as solid as this one, but I'm not aware of any secret entries. Let's see. It's on a slab, so there are no basement windows to give thee trouble."

Ruth thought a bit more, then shook her head. "I can't think of anything to suggest, except good locks.

And perhaps motion detectors."

She stood and crossed to the chest near the back door. "The key was in here," she said, pulling open a shallow top drawer. Several antique keys with ornate, filigreed bows lay in the drawer, along with some heavy padlocks from an earlier era.

I agreed that it made no sense to be concerned about a key that no longer opened anything. Ruth closed the drawer full of vintage keys and began to walk around the room, pointing out an oil lamp that she remembered from her earliest childhood, a framed photograph of her parents, another of her late husband, and a leather-bound copy of the sermons of Elias Hicks.

Hicks' cousin, Edward Hicks, was a notable primitive painter who lived and worked in Bucks County, and Ruth had what appeared to be an original Peaceable Kingdom hanging over the green velvet couch.

We stood in front of it, gazing at the oddly awkward wild animals, the distressingly unattractive children, and the ominous-looking brown snake coiled in the grass near its den in the river embankment.

"Edward Hicks didn't emphasize serpents in his Kingdoms," Ruth said, as she squinted at the painting, "although they're mentioned in the Isaiah verses he based the pictures on. And even when he did, they looked like garter snakes, harmless little things that wouldn't hurt the children.

"But this one looks threatening, don't you think? I wonder what Edward was thinking."

The painting appealed to me. I liked the lion lying down next to the lamb, the bear eating an ear of corn and looking not at all happy about it. I liked the innocence of the vision, and the devotion of the artist to the vision.

Ruth went to rescue the cookies and bring us tea. I looked out the window to the late summer trees beyond, their shuffling leaves rendered impressionistic by the wavy glass. After returning with a tray, she settled back onto the couch.

"Thy Lassiters were related to my husband's family," she said, pouring tea and handing me a cup. "I believe both families came across on the Whippet, one of the next ships after the Welcome. Which was lucky, considering most of the Welcome families were taken by smallpox before they even set foot in Pennsylvania."

"Wasn't Penn on the Welcome?" I asked, vaguely remembering family lore.

"Yes, that was his ship. My own Whitpaines were with him, but only the boy, Thomas, survived."

I knew my father said our family settled around Penn's time, but I didn't remember the details because, like most children, I didn't pay close attention. I wished I had.

We sipped tea and indulged in cinnamon cookies in comfortable silence. Then I remembered another thing I wanted to ask Ruth about. I described my flowering tree and asked her if she knew anything about it.

"Oh, yes! That's your Franklinia. It's a rare tree discovered by our own John Bartram, hundreds of years ago!"

"Our own who?"

"John Bartram. He was this country's first and foremost naturalist, during the 1700s. He went on collecting expeditions all over the colonies and identified many new species. He bred them in the gardens of his estate along the Schuylkill, near Philadelphia. We Quakers try to avoid excess pride, but we are proud of John Bartram.

"For the early Friends, the natural world was their passion. More so than other passions that people of leisure might have—art, or music. They were drawn to living things."

I thought about Uncle Elias, and the delight he always took in observing the beautiful detail in a puffball or bracket fungus. Even my father loved the earth and the way nature had shaped it.

My thoughts returned to the fragrant tree in my yard.

"How is it that I have one of these rare trees?"

"Well, that used to be ours, before we sold the plot to Elias. It's not that old; I think my father planted it from nursery stock. They're available commercially, although they're thought to be extinct in the wild.

"They hate being transplanted, so we were content to leave it with the new owner and admire it from afar. One of these days I might find another for my side yard."

It pleased me, somehow, that Ruth was content to admire my tree from afar. And it pleased me even more to think of her planning to plant a new tree.

I got up to go, and Ruth insisted on sending me off with some cookies. At the door, she paused and said, "Elias had some old letters, I think from John Bartram himself. Possibly other valuable documents. I doubt that he ever sold them, so they just might still be in thy house."

"Really? I haven't seen anything that looks valuable, but I'll take a closer look. There's just so much paper—I can't throw anything out without looking at every piece and trying to figure out what it is."

"Yes, I think that's wise. Some of those papers might be worth a bit."

As I waited, I took in the large room with fresh eyes. Something about its simple but ancient design, the burnished metal and glimmering stone, spoke to me. The scent of furniture wax and cinnamon made me think of long afternoons in the company of leather-bound books. Marta would approve.

****

I did a quick survey of my yard, looking for storm damage. Small branches and leaves littered the ground, but nothing serious had occurred. I glanced through the pines toward the river and was startled to find it had risen dramatically. The storm had churned up silt and the water looked like chocolate milk in the bright sunlight. A flotilla of tree limbs drifted past.

I turned my attention to paying bills, something I hate but do with obsessive care. I dread the idea of falling behind or having to deal with collection agencies.

Property taxes on the house hit twice a year; the August part was paid out of the estate before I took title, but I'd have another part to pay in the spring, along with the homeowner's insurance premium. Maintenance so far was fairly manageable—locks and a can of paint or two, but the water heater was unreliable. The pilot light tended to go out at inopportune moments, but I was afraid to call someone out, both for the cost of the visit and for the likely recommendation to buy a new unit.

With the features I was selling to the *Clarion*, I was managing, barely, to cover my expenses. I thought about creating a website to market my editing services—"Lassiter Literary," perhaps. I could hire Pradip to set it up, but I wasn't sure if a glass of Guinness would be quite enough to compensate him.

I had sent resumes to the larger papers within commuting distance, but not farther afield, as I didn't want to part with my free house. Someday I might consider that option, moving to some distant city and selling Uncle Elias' place. But for now, my plan was to try to make it in Fenton's Crossing.

The problem was, the bigger papers were shedding employees, not hiring them. And all the other places one might apply to as a freelancer, from old-time paper magazines to online sites, were paying next to nothing, or nothing at all. One website wrote back and offered to pay for content, but it had to be sponsored content, which amounted to advertising. I have nothing against advertising, as it's what supports publications, but that's not the kind of writing I do.

Oh, and content. I hate that word. The term is offensively neutral, meaning, I suppose, that it could be any kind of editorial copy: obituaries, police reports, features, wedding announcements. Good news, bad news, happy, sad. Well written or a grammatical shambles. So it comes to mean nothing at all. To the bean counters, apparently it means those little black squiggles that fill space between ads.

Chapter Thirteen

"Look at it this way," Kevin said, punching the cream-two-sugars button on the hot beverage machine. "At least he can't fire you."

"I don't know why not," I said, as Ezra and I watched Kevin's cup sputter full. "I feel like some kind of zombie. I'm dead, but here I am, filing stories like a regular live reporter."

Ezra fed his coins into the machine and bravely selected black coffee. "It's like, 'Screw you and the horse you rode in on,' " he said. " 'Oh, and can I borrow your horse?' "

We sat at one of the tired, peeling tables in the *Clarion* break room, avoiding the smudged table, with its big "Pressmen" sign. This was where the ink-stained men who ran the presses at night sat and had their coffee, and several naïve newcomers had sat down there, to their regret.

I'd dropped by the paper to pick up my check, which was faster than waiting for it to arrive in the mail. Matt Papiernik, the city editor, had waylaid me in the hall. He'd looked more disheveled than usual, his glasses smudged and a Lucky Strike tucked behind his ear.

"Miren! How's it going! Say, would you be able to cover a meeting tonight?"

"Matt, I was fired a few weeks ago. Does this mean

they're going to give me my old job back?"

He inched toward the exit as he spoke, eager to get outside where he could light up.

"Now, Miren. You weren't fired. We've always respected your work. It's just that Hampton Township called a special meeting. They might fire their township manager tonight. Frank is booked, and we really have to have someone there."

After laying off a third of the newsroom staff, management and the senior editors seemed amazed that buildings continued to burn, robbers continued to rob, cars crashed and the planning commission insisted on holding meetings.

Over and over, Matt had to pick up the phone and beg his former employees to work as stringers, doing piece work as independent contractors.

A few who were still collecting unemployment checks had told Matt and F.X. exactly where they could put their assignments. I, on the other hand, couldn't afford pride right now. Four stories would generate enough to cover my semi-annual car insurance premium

So I said yes, reluctantly, to Matt, and told the tale to Kevin and Ezra as they sipped their coffee.

Before I left, I went back in to the newsroom to see if Jodi was off the phone and had time to say hello. She was gripping her hair with both hands and making an anguished face.

"I can't stand it!" she groaned.

Jodi hooked a strand of her straight, dark red hair behind an ear and sighed heavily. Everything about her was disordered, from her desk to her blouse with its buttons out of sync, to her outfits that often looked as if she grabbed something out of the dryer and dressed in the dark. And yet, she managed her department, fought for her turf, supported her people, filled her pages with lively and relevant and useful stories. And she was raising four children, as well.

She had edited one of June Snodgrass' columns a few days ago, and added some transitional phrases without which the column made no sense at all. A few minutes ago, she had seen June march into F.X.'s office, this morning's edition in hand. Jodi awaited her fate.

"Listen to this!" She began to read from the raw copy June had submitted

I tried to shush her. "Jeez, Jodi! Don't let her hear you! You have to be all innocent about this!"

" 'Halloween is almost here,' " she read. " 'so Betty Satterthwaite has to take Fluffy to the vet this week.' "

"She never says what Fluffy's vet visit has to do with Halloween! She never even tells us what kind of animal Fluffy is! Dog? Cat? Bunny? Madagascar Hissing Cockroach? This is the kind of writing that makes sense only to the person who wrote it, and to no one else. That's not what newspapers are supposed to do!" Her voice rose to a squeal.

I assured her that *Clarion* readers had survived fifty years of June's stylings, and would continue to survive happily as long as June put their names in the paper. But like all good editors, Jodi felt responsible for everything that appeared on her pages, and to carry that responsibility with no control is torture.

I have never quite understood writers who get all huffy if their copy is changed. Of course it depends on the editor—some can wreak havoc on a story. But a good editor makes your stories better and saves your bacon when you make a mistake.

Jodi rarely changed my copy. She accepted my spelling of proper names, knowing I had double checked them. She trusted me, and I trusted her to run my copy through her skilled fingers, feeling for little knots and snags. What she did change made my stories read better and made me look good.

I saw the door to F.X.'s office open, and before June could emerge, I gave Jodi a pat on the shoulder and abandoned her to her fate. I headed for the employees' exit next to the loading dock and picked my way through the cigarette butts toward the parking lot.

A thin young man with a metallic silver backpack walked along the tracks, heading south. I thought about the Amtrak Acela that sometimes swept past on that track. I had a brief frisson of worry for his safety.

As I unlocked my car door, I saw that he'd turned back and was crossing the parking lot toward me.

I paused and turned toward him. He was very young, with a bit of acne still holding its own against the new stubble on his cheek. He looked vaguely familiar.

"Excuse me," he began. Just then, the door to a nondescript gray Taurus opened, and Mark Calabrese unfolded his six-foot-plus frame, climbed out and ambled over.

The stranger whirled around and retreated toward the tracks, disappearing behind a *Clarion* delivery van.

"Can't stay away, can you?" Mark said with a grin.

My gaze lingered briefly on the van before turning toward Mark.

"It kills me to do it," I said, "but I can't afford to turn anything down. I'm heading for the Hampton meeting tonight, from which I expect to garner sixteen inches and a modest check. And you? How are you managing? You didn't fill me in on moving day."

When I think about the decline of traditional newspapers, I worry about the decline of Mark and other investigative reporters. The *Clarion* had kept Mark on, but I wondered how long that would last. Over the years, he had exposed municipal corruption, revealed scam artists who pretended to be war heroes, uncovered odometer rollbacks and employers who neglected to pay their employees. Sometimes law enforcement was ineffective. Politicians weren't interested. Mark had exposed wrongdoing because nobody else would do it. That's what a newspaper can do, and I can only hope that whatever replaces it can still do it.

It's expensive, paying a salary to a reporter who doesn't generate any copy for weeks as he builds a story. Plus legal fees and kerfuffle and canceled subscriptions when someone's ox is gored. Far cheaper and easier to focus on bake sales and cute weather pictures. I hoped the *Clarion* was sticking with its investigative role because it served a purpose, and management hadn't figured out a way to get it for free.

Without a local newspaper, corruption is too easy. When a feisty reporter is sniffing at your heels, it's a lot harder. I suspect there are people who watch the asphyxiation of newspapers and rub their hands together in glee.

I was pleased to hear Mark say he thought his job was secure. "I have too many unfinished projects for them to let me go at this point," he said. "My plan is to keep them tantalized, like Scheherazade. Oh, by the way…"

His genial face turned solemn, and he reached into his pocket. "I was in your ancestral home on vacation. Took some awesome video of the mountains and salt flats. They'll make you homesick. No big deal, but why don't you hang on to it."

He handed me a bronze-colored flash drive. This seemed a bit cloak-and-daggery to me; there must be something else on the drive that he didn't want to mention. I looked at him quizzically but figured he must have his reasons. I took the drive and tucked it into my shoulder bag.

I checked my watch and decided to go back into the building with Mark. It was getting a bit late to go home and then come back for the meeting, so I'd do a quick check of the files to figure out what was going on with the Hampton manager. Whatever happened tonight, it was likely to appear on page one in the morning, with my name on it. I intended to do my homework.

After that, I headed out to McLipids for a Double Whammy with Cheese. Weighted down with fast food and worries, I headed over to the township building. The meeting was interminable and inconclusive. Nobody was fired. Warring factions on the board of supervisors carped at one another for several hours, then adjourned.

I grabbed a few township officials for quotes and tried to probe them for any hints about what was really going on. Then I called the desk and relayed the news that the story wasn't likely to merit page one, but I thought I could give them about ten inches, such as it was. I was only a few miles away, so I went back to the *Clarion* to file.

I had to press the buzzer at the night entrance and wait for a security guard to let me in. After a while, Gil Martinez appeared in his security uniform, recognized me through the window, and opened up.

The newsroom smelled of coffee and someone's greasy night lunch. It had a sleepy, yet uneasy feel; the skeleton crew was hoping all the late stories would come in on time and that everything would fit. Hoping nothing blew up anywhere in the world before quitting time.

Mandy was on the night desk, overseeing the few reporters hunched over their computers, tapping out late stories. A few were on the phone, desperate to track down that last quote the story required.

Only the copy desk seemed relaxed, waiting for the late copy to pour in. They sat leaning back in their chairs in the official swing-shift uniform of T-shirts and flip-flops. Ray was playing Spider Solitaire, and Megan, ever dutiful, was browsing through the AP Stylebook.

I grabbed a desk and finished my story. I checked to make sure Mandy had my cell number in case of questions and headed out the door.

It was close to midnight when I finally pulled into the driveway. I hadn't remembered to turn on my porch light, so I fumbled with my keys. I must have tried to open the door with my car key, because it didn't work. It made a metallic, scraping sound.

I found the right one and went inside, turning on lights, as something flickered in my memory. That sound. I'd heard it before, the sound of someone trying the wrong key. An insistent metallic crunching.

I'd heard it just before the power went out, shortly after I'd moved in. I'd just had the locks changed, and a good thing, too. Someone had been using Elias' old key to try to get into my house.

Chapter Fourteen

.

"Homicide." Spencer's voice sounded crackly on my cell.

"Really?" I moved closer to the kitchen window, hoping for better reception.

"Yep. The medical examiner is calling a press conference this afternoon to announce it."

I exhaled. "Wow. So his widow was right. He didn't hang himself."

"No, he didn't. That would have been hard, since he was dead before he was strung up on the gallows."

I had been tidying the kitchen counter while on the phone; I stopped short.

"Someone strangled him first?" I could picture Spencer nodding.

"And hung him from the gallows, in the hope of making it look like suicide," he said.

"So now your story switches from What Happened to Whodunit," I said. "Guess you'll be able to keep it for a while longer."

At the *Clarion*, the police reporter covered crimes and accidents at the local level. The story was Spencer's until a suspect was identified and bound over for trial. Then the court reporter would take over.

"You'll probably hear from them," Spencer said. "They're going to have to re-interview everyone who was at the museum that morning."

****

After the chilly thunderstorm that cut our power early in September, the weather settled into a late summer lassitude where days were hot and steamy, but nights fell like a dark curtain and sent people searching through their off-season closets for sweaters.

Then October came, and it seemed as if a spell had broken and the real world revealed. A pall of humidity lifted. Annoying gnats and mosquitoes disappeared. Colors shone more brightly, and sounds carried more clearly. Canada geese took to the skies where they honked and made V formations, but never actually left for southern climes. Pumpkins and chrysanthemums tumbled from markets and roadside stands.

The crisp, dry air felt like home to me. The warmth of the sun flipped to chill when I walked from sunlight to shade, just as it had in the high desert. But in Nevada, trees were a rare species in the dry flat regions. In the mountains, they were mostly evergreens, certainly welcome in winter but not much to celebrate in the fall.

Only the aspens provided their color. In Pennsylvania's wooded hills and valleys, the trees turned bronze, brass, gold, and every possible alloy, along with scarlet and many varieties of wine.

The exhilarating weather boosted my energy, and my output. By mid-October, I had filed a story on an emergency meeting of the Walpole Township Municipal Sewer Authority, an interview with an elderly piano teacher who had once taught somebody famous, and a profile on an author of a book about the writers who had made Bucks County their home in the early twentieth century. The sheer talent was quite remarkable: native son James Michener, and transplants Dorothy Parker, George F. Kaufman, Pearl Buck and others.

This morning's task was to set up an interview with a Kingston University professor who had had an unfortunate run-in with people hostile to the idea of climate change. Aaron Caldwell had been accused of tweaking temperature data to make his case. Because he commuted from his home in Bucks County, the *Clarion* considered him local, and worth a profile.

I called and asked if he would be available for an interview about his work and recent events. He hemmed for a while, and I quickly tried to snag him with a commitment by suggesting the following Wednesday or Thursday afternoon. Once Caldwell was offered specifics, he was energized in his efforts to explain how that just wouldn't do.

"Let's see. Wednesday I'm giving a guest lecture at Rutgers, and Thursday I'm accepting an award from the American Meteorological Association. Friday, I have some peer reviews due, and next Monday I'm expected to…

It's always baffled me why people have to explain their entire schedule before indicating availability, flaunting their busy calendars like Rolexes.

I asked if he could suggest a time, and after a bit more preening about how busy and interesting he was, Caldwell finally settled on two p.m. the following Tuesday. He gave directions to his office and we hung up.

It was nearly mid-morning when I laced my walking shoes and headed out the front door. I'd seen Melanie Butterfield from my window, out in her garden doing something with straw. I wandered over to see what was up. I was becoming downright chatty and neighborly, I thought. What was happening to my reclusive, curmudgeonly demeanor?

"Hi, Miren." Melanie said, straightening up, and brushing straw off her hands. "We're hoping for some fall lettuce and peas. If we succeed, you'll have to try some."

I bent down and examined the rows. The lettuce was thriving. Pea plants, cute as little puppies, were about six inches tall and sending off tendrils. "Aw," I said. "They're looking for something to grab!"

"Oh, I'll give them chicken wire this weekend. I'm just hoping we can harvest a crop before hard frost. They'll probably be okay until mid-November. The lettuce we can cover with glass, so I know we'll get a good bit."

How Melanie could add organic gardening to her long list of tasks was a mystery, but I maintained my usual diplomatic silence. I said goodbye and headed for the towpath.

The canal had fallen on hard times since its heyday in the mid-nineteenth century. Rescued from complete oblivion in the 1970s, the canal was now a state park— certainly the longest and narrowest of parks—and struggled mightily for enough funding to keep from silting up altogether.

I headed north and fell into a satisfying stride. My hips and flanks flexed, feet pressing against the earth as though pushing the globe in its rotation. I was in the zone; as an invisible force propelled me forward, one thought grasped another, like links in a chain, knots in a braid. I thought about toothbrushes and house keys. I thought about Graham Farnsworth and his enemies. I thought about whatever data was on Mark's thumb drive.

The parcel just north of my property line was wooded; someone had told me it belonged to Ruth Lovering. When they sold my piece to Elias, they kept that to preserve their riparian rights and access to the river.

Beyond that, some backyards were open to the towpath, others screened with hedges or fences. I enjoyed gazing at the private face of people's property as I swung past. Soon, however, dwellings gave way to woods, and I walked in solitude. Leaves were beginning to drift from the trees.

I sniffed the aroma of moisture and chlorophyll that marks the woods in Pennsylvania, and detected a faint undertone of horse manure, suggesting someone nearby had a farm. I contrasted this with the scents of my childhood, layered with sage and resinous plants whose acrid aromas spoke of the closed pores of the high desert flora.

On my right, the woods gave way to a split rail fence, and in the field beyond, two dark chestnut horses grazed. A copse of trees partially obscured a dwelling in the distance; after a few minutes I was able to make out the corner of a stone house, not unlike Ruth Lovering's. Nearby was a bank barn, with the earth graded up to the entrance like a steep driveway. A cottage and what looked like a long, grape-festooned pergola glowed in the distance. I walked for about five minutes before I came to the wooden fence that marked the other boundary of the property. That was one generous parcel, at least by eastern standards.

On the other side of the fence, about a dozen sheep stood, all staring at me as though I was some otherworldly creature. Most were dirty white, with their puffy bodies balanced on dark, skinny legs. One had chocolate brown fleece. They chewed thoughtfully as I walked by, following my progress with their eyes.

These must be the sheep Marta had mentioned as the source of her wool. They were smaller than the ones I remember from my childhood, when we visited my grandfather out near Winnemucca. Those were tougher, shaggier animals than these, a breed suited to the bitter climate and scant plant life.

My grandfather had it easier than his own father, but life was still harsh. The appeal of sleeping in a proper bunkhouse, putting in a day's work and then coming home to a hearty family-style meal cooked by girls from the old country, must have been irresistible. Naturally, he married the cook.

I never met my grandmother, but I inherited a few things from her. First, I'm a pretty good cook. If called upon, I could create a hearty meal for a dozen people with my eyes closed. Living alone, I don't get much opportunity to demonstrate that talent.

I also have her first name, which is a Basque version of Mary.

As cattle ranchers moved in, my great-grandfather's way of life changed. Range wars between sheep and cattlemen broke out, and the open range was fenced and "privatized."

My grandfather grew up with a great resentment toward cattlemen, whom he considered arrogant and greedy. But it was more than that: he felt disrespected, as of course he was.

As long as I knew him, he never ate beef.

I remembered once, when I was maybe eight, we visited him as he was preparing to move out of his ranch house and into an apartment in town. Needless to say, it wasn't an easy process for him, but he accepted that it had to be done. That afternoon, while his daughter and son-in-law packed and labeled boxes, he put me and Rab, his sheepdog, in the truck and drove out to the back country.

He parked next to a boulder field. We got out, and he led me back through pines and scrub, along a gravel gully. Rab ran wildly up the trail and back, hoping to find some sheep to herd. Soon, my grandfather stopped and looked around, and I could tell memories were flooding into his mind. He pointed off to one side. All I saw was a pile of rocks, almost as tall as me. Clearly someone had arranged it for a purpose.

"That's a stone boy," he told me. "We made them to mark trails or tell us which way to go for water. Not sure why they're called that. Maybe because they're about the size of a boy." He looked down at me, and his dark eyes softened. "Or maybe a girl.

"Of course, in the old days, we called them *harrimutilak*. My father said they had 'em back in the Basque country. It's dry and stony in parts over there, especially in the mountains."

He fell silent, which was his habit. I crouched down and collected pebbles. And then he whistled for Rab, turned and led me down the trail to the truck.

Chapter Fifteen

On Thursday, I made a trip to the thrift shop with several cartons of housewares and clothing, along with a few lamps and a small table I knew I wouldn't use. I handed my stuff across the counter, and the clerk gave me a receipt. I knew I was unlikely to benefit much from my charitable donation, being poor and all, but I took it. You never know. I might win the lottery and find myself in a higher tax bracket.

On the way out, I stopped by a rack of blouses. As I've said, I'm not much of a shopper. But a shimmery copper-colored blouse caught my eye. The price was three dollars. I held it up to myself in front of the mirror, declared it acceptable, paid, and left.

I found myself in good spirits on the drive home. Clearing out clutter is a good feeling. Once I figured out what to do with Elias' botanical items and scientific instruments, I'd really be de-junked.

I was thinking pleasant thoughts about Marta's decorating insights when I unlocked my door and walked into the living room.

I stopped short.

Something about a house is different when there's another person breathing in it. As soon as I stepped through the door, I knew someone was in the house. Something was different. A smell, a sound, the absence of an expected sound, something.

When I set it down, the bag from the thrift shop made a crinkling sound that seemed alarmingly loud. I moved stealthily toward the kitchen and quietly slid a knife from the drawer. I checked that my phone was in my pocket.

No one was on the first floor; that was evident. If anyone was upstairs, he or she was at a decided disadvantage. I stood still and raised my eyes to the loft railing. Nothing. No sign of movement.

I began the slow, silent climb up the stairs, staying on the outside edge where squeaks were less likely. A shudder ran down my arms, lifting the hair, holding up the fabric of my shirt like a picnic cloth on dry grass. When my eyes were level with the loft floor, I surveyed the room.

Someone was in the bed.

The blanket was lumped, with more bulk than a simple unmade bed could generate. I thought briefly about backing down the stairs and calling the police, but that would take time and possibly lead to embarrassment.

I climbed the remaining steps and stood on the top one, the knife behind my back. "Who are you?"

The blanket stirred and a startled figure sat up.

It was the thin kid. The metallic backpack lay on the floor beside the bed.

"Who are you," I asked again, "and what are you doing in my house?"

The boy stared, not quite awake. He seemed to be having trouble forming words.

"I...I'm sorry. I shouldn't have come in. I'll leave." He started to stand, then sat back down, reaching for worn sneakers.

"Yes, I expect you to leave, but I want you to tell me who you are and why you're here."

"I had to see where you lived. I had to talk to you. I was so tired. I fell asleep." He fumbled with the gray, worn shoelaces.

"Do you have a name?"

He looked at me with an expression of ancient pain, so odd on a youthful face with just the beginning of a beard.

"You don't know who I am, do you." It was a statement, not a question.

"No, I don't know who you are."

He tied the second lace and slowly rose to his feet.

"I'm your son."

Chapter Sixteen

What he'd said was nonsensical. I brandished my phone. "Look, one click and the police will be here in a matter of minutes."

"Will you at least listen to what I have to say?"

I don't know why I found myself wanting to hear his story. Something about his vulnerability made him unthreatening. I knew he was wrong. But I wanted to hear why he chose to believe something impossible.

"You're mistaken, but I'll listen. Somewhere else. Not here, in my bedroom. Not in my house. How did you get in here?"

He said nothing. I backed down the stairs so I could keep him in my sight. I still had the knife and phone at the ready. He followed, his pack hanging from one hand. I led him outside and around to the back yard. We went through the pines down the slope to the river bank.

A flat rock, reddish brown, jutted out from the bank and made a long, uneven bench. We sat, side by side, but facing away from each other. He looked downstream, I upstream.

"My name is Miren, but I assume you know that already. Why don't you start by telling me your name."

"It's Seth."

He couldn't have been more than nineteen or twenty. He had several days' worth of stubble on his chin and upper lip, but elsewhere his pale cheeks bore only the faint scars of recent acne.

His eyes were blue, the cloudy color that new kittens have when they first open their eyes. "Seth, you need to know this. I don't have any children."

I watched the water move toward me, patiently working its way from the mountains of New York. Seth watched the water move toward Delaware Bay and the sea.

I sensed him near me and sensed his waiting. I felt the familiar welling up of words, words I didn't want to speak. They rose within me, without my will or guidance, and flowed the only direction they could, toward my mouth.

"I did have a baby," I began. "A long time ago, but he was born dead.

"I was seventeen, living in what amounts to a commune. I didn't want any of what they made me do, including having a baby. Of course I was expected to give birth at home, if you can call it home. No real doctor, no drugs.

"When it was over, they gave him to me to hold. He was gray, not pink. So quiet. But he was beautiful, perfect. He was still warm. From me, not from his own life. I held him until he was cold."

The water slid by, left to right, orderly. I wondered what it was like to live on the Jersey side and grow up accustomed to a counter-clockwise river. My mind skittered to right-to-left scripts, like Hebrew, and I felt the familiar warning bell telling me my thoughts were running off the rails.

Seth was silent for a long time. He had been picking at an edge of shale on the side of the rock, and a layer separated in his hand. He tossed it into the river.

"Do you remember the date?"

"I will never forget it."

He hitched to one side and reached into his back pocket for a frayed, soiled wallet. He pulled out a driver's license and handed it to me.

It was a Nevada license. It had his name, Seth Morrow, a Reno address, and his date of birth. The November date that had been bringing me down for twenty years. I looked at his face. Something odd happened to my inside. None of this made any sense. And yet, I didn't find myself pushing him away.

"Is there any way you could be mistaken about what happened?" he said. "You were very young, and you had the baby in a pretty scary situation."

"If he had been alive, even for a minute, I would have known. Dead babies don't come back to life. And your having the same birthday doesn't mean anything."

"Were you married?"

"Yes and no. I was living in a place where marriages were arranged outside the legal system."

His questions felt like pressure on an incision that still ached. I had built a sturdy wall blocking off that part of my past and had no interest in demolition.

He looked at me as though wondering if he could push me a bit more, then thought better of it.

He began to speak, starting with his earliest life, growing up as a favored son of Elder Morrow at the compound in northern Nevada, but without a mother. He'd been told his mother had died, and Morrow's other wives—-whom he called his aunts—raised him.

"After the compound was dissolved, the county put me in a foster home. They were pretty good; I got along with the family and did okay in school. But then I turned eighteen and would have aged out, except I was still a senior so I was able to stay until I graduated.

"I asked them if they knew anything about my parents, but they didn't. So after I left, I found the compound on a map and drove out there. It was a ghost town. Just what you'd expect: tumbleweeds, rusty chain link fences. I checked the newspaper articles and found out Elder Morrow is still in prison. Other than him, I couldn't find anybody. Everybody scattered. There was nobody to ask."

Above us, a hawk circled. We watched as it made several slow revolutions, then moved off. Seth continued. "One of the articles referred to a girl who had escaped from the compound years earlier. I became curious; it was right about the time I was born. I fantasized that my mother was still alive somewhere.

"There was a kid from the compound named Abel, who I kept in touch with. He remembered hearing stories about how two of Elder Morrow's wives had disappeared. One was before I was born, and he remembered her name. Estelle Lassiter.

"He thought the other one was her daughter. That gave me a last name. A little searching online and a little hitchhiking brought me here."

The birthday, the last name, the other parts of his story made his surmise plausible—at least to him. I studied his eyes, his facial features, as if that mattered since we couldn't possibly be related.

And yet, we had a lot in common, if he was telling the truth. We had each lived at the compound and been linked to Elder Morrow. Each, in our own way, was a lost soul.

"Well, you found me. And I'm not your mother. It's pretty clear that we have a connection to the compound. I wish you the best, really, but your search for your mother has to go in a different direction."

His downcast look made me feel ridiculously guilty. What was I supposed to do, just declare him my son, even if he wasn't? Adopt him?

I tried to regain my composure. I tried to sound stern. "Mind telling me how you got into my house?"

He sighed and rummaged in his backpack. He pulled out what looked and sounded like a key chain, but instead of keys, long thin pieces of flat metal dangled from it.

"If someone wanted to do that, they would use something like these," he said. "Especially someone who did it as a kid and got pretty good at it."

My voice rose. "You picked my lock?"

"I apologize for going into your house," he said. He stood up, unfolding his lean form to what seemed like a great height to me. I scrambled to my feet and wondered where I'd left the knife.

He started up the bank, toward my yard.

I followed him. Again, my mouth took the lead. "Where are you living?"

He was heading across the lawn toward the towpath. He turned and said, "I'd rather not say." He pushed through the shrubs that screened the towpath, then turned back and said, "I've been doing some work for the guy who runs the pub down on the highway. Desmond. If for any reason you want to get in touch with me, you can leave a message with him."

There was a pause. Then he said, "I would recommend dead-bolts."

And he was gone.

****

From the archives of the *The Elk City Echo*
October 19, 2005

Seven Arrested in Raid on Cult Compound

(AP) Authorities raided a compound in rural Pershing County Tuesday morning and arrested seven adults on suspicion of firearms violations, terroristic threats, and child endangerment, officials said.

According to the county sheriff's department, a joint team of sheriff deputies and U.S. Treasury Department agents surrounded the compound near Route 14 shortly before dawn. They said shots were fired from inside the compound, but no injuries were reported and the suspects eventually surrendered peacefully.

Arrested were Benjamin Morrow, 49, his wife Rebecca Morrow, 47, Barbara Morrow, 45, Melissa Morrow, 28, and three others whom authorities did not name because it was not clear if they were minors, authorities said.

It was not immediately clear what relationship the younger Morrows were to Benjamin and Rebecca. Several children, including an infant, were also taken into custody and placed with county protective services.

The compound has been a concern for authorities for more than a decade, with reports of child marriages, kidnapping and possible terrorist activities, officials said. Local and state police have complained of receiving threatening letters from residents of the compound.

Authorities said the adults are being held in the county jail in Lovelock awaiting arraignment.

Chapter Seventeen

I briefly considered sleeping on the loveseat, but concluded I'd have to face the bed my intruder had slept in eventually. I stripped the bedding and put on fresh sheets, then fell, exhausted, into a half sleep haunted by half dreams.

I woke at dawn on Tuesday to the familiar sound of gravel crunching. I got up and looked out my south windows, toward the shared driveway.

Simeon Kempe had pushed his huge motorcycle from its shed and was wheeling it laboriously down the drive. When he reached the pavement, he stopped, slipped on his helmet, and started the engine. Once it caught, he kept it throttled down, then eased into the road and away.

To all appearances, Simeon was courtesy personified, going out of his way to avoid disturbing his sleeping neighbors. I realized I knew very little about him, other than his biker appearance.

After coffee and breakfast, I started laundry and sat down with my laptop to dig up a bit of background on Aaron Caldwell and his work. I checked the university's website and found the location of the Atmospheric and Oceanic Sciences Department and Caldwell's lab.

I gathered my notebook and phone, dispensing with my camera. If Jodi wanted a photo, she could set one up later. I drove along the river to New Hope and crossed the bridge into Lambertville. From there, I cut across woods and fields that made me forget I was in New Jersey. Gradually, the landscape filled with strip malls and housing developments, and soon I was crossing the thundering traffic of Route 1 and pulling into a parking lot outside Dr. Caldwell's building.

Because I was writing a feature, I intended to go light on the science, and concentrate most on Caldwell as a local kid from Levittown who'd made news. *Clarion* readers didn't want to get too deep into the atmospheric weeds, but I had to gain an understanding of his work in order to explain it clearly to my readers.

Caldwell welcomed me more graciously than I had expected, given his self-importance during our efforts to schedule an appointment. I asked him if he had any objections to my recording the interview, and he said I was welcome to. I rarely use a recorder, relying on my fast and brutal handwriting, but I always record anything that might be controversial. I also take paper notes, and usually keep the tape as a backup. I figured under the circumstances, Caldwell would appreciate an accurate record.

He was eager to talk about the controversy. It seemed he had been collaborating with a British university in assembling climate data from numerous studies, adding up to thousands of years of information about world temperatures. Putting this unwieldy information into comprehensible graphs and charts required shortcuts well-established in science, but that could seem suspicious to the layman.

Caldwell preferred to imply that his adversaries had simply misunderstood scientific techniques, but the fact that they had hacked his email, while politicians had seized on the controversy to discredit the foundations of climate change research, suggested an agenda.

A Texas congressman had subpoenaed his records, and a movement was building to have him dismissed for falsifying data.

Whatever the motivations, the inspectors general of several respected scientific agencies had reviewed the situation and just announced that they cleared Caldwell of all charges of falsifying or manipulating data.

"Their conclusions were unambiguous," he said. "It was clear that the charges were baseless. We knew that, of course, but it was very satisfying to be vindicated."

As Caldwell warmed to his topic, he became more human and less determined to make an impression. He opened file drawers and showed me charts and notes. He reached behind his chair to a credenza where huge slabs of tree trunks, with their rings carefully labeled, demonstrated changes in the environment over centuries. Next to the tree rings was a framed photo. It was taken in England, and showed him with two colleagues, smiling happily in front of an ancient brick academic building.

We talked about the possible motives of his accusers, and then I asked Caldwell what motives they attributed to him. "What possible reason would you have for falsifying data?" I asked.

"They claim we do it for the grant money—to get rich!" He chuckled mordantly. "The other side is funded by the energy industry. There's no counterpart in science. Either they're projecting, assuming we all are driven by greed, or they know perfectly well that's not true, but say it anyway."

I shifted the interview to more personal matters. Caldwell chatted happily about his family, his dog, his fondness for camping in the Pine Barrens in the southern part of New Jersey.

As the interview wound down, he asked politely about my work. I explained that I was working freelance for the *Clarion* and had recently moved into a house I inherited from my uncle.

Suddenly he looked as though a light bulb had just switched on above his head.

"My god, are you related to Elias Lassiter?" he asked. "He and I consulted sometimes, about interesting things he was observing about habitat changes. His death was a loss to science, as well as to his friends and family."

He was silent for a while. "He also worked closely with a geneticist named Stephen Melchior. Do you know him?"

I didn't. I explained I knew very little about my uncle's work and colleagues but would like to know more.

Caldwell looked at his watch. He was, I recalled, a busy man. I disconnected the tape recorder and tucked my notebook into my shoulder bag and made leaving motions. But he waved me back into my seat.

"Let me give you Steve's email. He really liked your uncle. I'm sure he'd be glad to hear from you."

****

I pulled into the driveway and stopped to pick up the mail. I found an ad for flooring, a credit card offer, and an envelope with my name handwritten on the front. It had no postmark or stamp; someone must have hand delivered it.

Back in the kitchen, I opened the letter.

Dear Ms. Lassiter,

My name is Lawrence Shaw. My late father, Eugene Shaw, was a colleague of your great-uncle. I want to extend my condolences to you on the loss of your uncle, whom I knew slightly. My father thought very highly of him and considered him a friend.

I am a collector of old and obsolete laboratory equipment. If you should decide that you want to part with any of your uncle's equipment, would you consider letting me look at it? Such items are rarely valuable, but I would offer a fair price for anything you might sell me.

The signature was followed by an email address and a phone number whose prefix suggested that Mr. Shaw lived in the upper part of the county.

My first thought was that it would be good to find a home for my uncle's possessions, and having a ready buyer was a good thing. But then I concluded I didn't feel quite ready yet to clear everything out, especially things I hadn't yet properly identified. I put the letter in the growing pile of mail and papers that I didn't feel like dealing with right away.

****

The next morning, I spread out my notes from the Caldwell interview on the desk. I wanted to list the points I planned to include in a rough outline and went in search of scratch paper.

I remembered that the lower drawer of one of Elias' file cabinets contained a jumble of stationery and office supplies, and I rummaged through all manner of

117

legal pads, quadrille tablets, yellow second sheets and a few notepads. The paper seemed older and more yellow around the edges the deeper I dug.

I lifted a sheet of relatively new, white paper to reveal a hand-written letter, the paper discolored to a buff tone, and the ink faded. Another blank sheet protected the second letter, and so on. Perhaps a dozen old letters lay there, each sandwiched between clean sheets.

I held the first one up in the light. It had hard creases where it had been folded long ago.

It was addressed to John Bartram, Philadelphia, thanking him for his letter about his exploration of forests near the Ohio River. It was dated February 1744.

It was signed, "Benj. Franklin," with the final "n" ending in a swoop of loops that curled under the name. I felt my heart skip a beat. Could this be genuine?

I lifted the next sheet, and the next. Several letters were addressed to Mordecai Lassiter and signed, "John Bartram." They appeared to be cover letters for shipments of plants.

One of Bartram's letters enthusiastically described a new species of moss that he'd discovered in Virginia. Presumably the letters had been passed down through my family, from Mordecai to Elias. One of them began:

My steadfast Friend Mordecai,

I take this oppty to thank you for your support in my endeavour to confront the Hessians in Trenton. I know you will not partake of the act of war, and yearn for all to live at Peace, but you have bade me follow my own counsel in this matter, and considering the Calumny heap'd upon me by our neighbors, I have found your kindness a great Comfort."

It continued in this vein, and was signed, "Eliphalet Fenton."

Were these letters what my intruders were after? Why they would take my toothbrush and leave all the papers unmolested didn't make sense, but then, nothing did.

It might be time to find a safer home for the documents, but I didn't feel like buying a safe or and renting a safe deposit box just for this. Perhaps Edmond Greenwood would keep them for me. I carefully replaced the letters where I'd found them. Their hiding place had seemed safe enough thus far.

I turned my attention back to my story. Jody had asked for twenty-two inches by eleven this morning. As I jotted down notes, I thought about what I needed to do in a feature about a scientist. I try to strike a careful balance between my lede and my subject in a feature. A highly technical story may require a lighter note at the beginning, as a way of drawing readers in (or at least not scaring them off). But there wasn't much light about Dr. Caldwell's travails.

I did what I always did when unsure how to begin: I had a cup of coffee. This would be a great time for a cigarette, if I smoked. I surfed my favorite websites, then wandered into my blog comment community.

Basquette Case: Morning, all. Just a drive-by while I await inspiration.

Grendel: May I be of help? Gotz inspiration to spare.

Basquette Case: Probably not. Got a climate scientist who was flamed by the deniers and has just been vindicated. Can't decide how technical to get.

Grendel: Never worked for a newspaper, but did PR for a university, lo these many years. For a general audience, I'd Keep It Simple Stupid. You're not a science writer, correct?

Basquette Case: Nope. Features. Human interest is what they want. What it feels like to have your feelings hurt by climate skeptics. But that doesn't seem like enough, somehow.

Grendel: You could always talk about how cold it was last winter, so how can the planet be getting warmer, huh?? Explain that, Mr. Smartypants!

After a bit of back and forth, I said farewell and signed off.

The last thing I wanted to do when I had an hour to write a story and no idea how to begin was to concentrate too hard on my lede. I didn't even like the term; it should be "lead," meaning lead paragraph. The odd spelling was meant to distinguish it from the metal lead, used in early typesetting.

For me, the trick to finding my lede is to not try too hard. It's like looking at stars. One of my favorite things about camping as a child was sleeping outside, looking up from my sleeping bag at the unobstructed universe. In the West, it's not hard to find places where light pollution doesn't exist. It's so dark at night that the stars are more than just visible; they illuminate the night.

On one of those occasions, my father sat next to me as I fell asleep and talked about the stars. He identified the Big Dipper and asked me if I could see a faint star he called Mizar.

I couldn't, at first, so he taught me how to look at a point slightly to the side of where it should be, and how that often helped a faint object come into view. Foveal vision, I now know it's called.

If I'm struggling with a lede, I sometimes use foveal techniques. If I'm fretful about my deadline and how little time I have left to think of something, I go blank. But if I relax and allow my mind to shift just a bit, the words come into focus.

And sure enough, after a few minutes I was rewarded. I opened a new document and began,

January 15 was a cold day in hell for Kingston climate scientist Aaron Caldwell.

The Northeast was experiencing the worst blizzard in more than a decade, and he knew he'd be fingered, sooner or later, by climate change deniers who were after his scalp...

The deep freeze only grew worse. Soon Caldwell, who had mapped data from millennia documenting that the earth was warming, was accused of fudging, or even inventing, his data. Calls for his firing mounted, and Congressional subpoenas arrived.

Once I had the lede, the next twenty inches followed logically. I like to think that my clumsiness— my tendency to get snagged on every obstruction in my physical world—is related to my ability to write effortlessly. The same trait that makes me trip, and tangle, and snarl at the slightest contact with coils and hooks also causes my brain to hook and connect one perception to another, leading me from one thought to another until I have a serviceable draft. The rest is simple editing.

By ten thirty, I'd attached the file to an email and shipped it off to Jodi.

I went back to *WonkLikeMe* to see if Grendel was

still there so I could thank him for the inspiration, but he appeared to have left. I scrolled back and saw that Flora was outraged about an op-ed in the New York Times, so much so that you could almost hear the sputtering through the screen. Mrs. Calabash was going out the door to a root canal appointment, and Rapscallion's brother had been laid off.

While I still had my notes spread out, I dug through them and found the email address Caldwell had given me for Stephen Melchior. I composed what I hoped was a polite message, identifying myself and saying that Caldwell had suggested I contact him to talk about my uncle's work. It seemed worth a try. No great loss if he wasn't interested in getting in touch.

Chapter Eighteen

On Friday morning, I went to Doylestown to be interviewed again about finding Graham Farnsworth's body. I'd notified Jodi, and she had said F.X. wanted to send the *Clarion*'s counsel to be present during the interview, just as a precaution.

Detective Parnell met me in the lobby and ushered me into an interview room. He said he'd been informed that Abraham Wilberforce, the *Clarion*'s lawyer, was on his way. We made small talk about the weather until Parnell's phone signaled the lawyer's arrival. He excused himself, and a moment later returned with a large, out-of-breath black man who seemed to fill the room. He apologized for his lateness and slammed his briefcase down on the desk.

I'd seen him at the *Clarion* from time to time, barging through the newsroom like an ocean liner. He'd nod and greet familiar reporters before heading to F.X.'s office and banging the door closed behind him. There, they would confer as controversial stories were readied for publication. Wilberforce had a reputation for caution when it came to media law, but an easy—sometimes edgy—manner in casual situations. He was also known for vivid neckties. This one, in silky cantaloupe, was relatively subdued.

Parnell took our coffee orders and left the room.

"I doubt this will take long," Wilberforce said,

snapping open his briefcase. "I'll just be here in case this guy asks questions that are over the line. I don't think that'll happen, so my plan is to take it easy and drink my coffee."

Detective Parnell returned, put the foam coffee cups down, and pushed some buttons on sound equipment on a side table. His questions were routine, primarily about what I had seen and what, if anything, I had touched at the scene. I told him I hadn't touched anything except the ladder and Millicent Pleat's shoulder.

We were finished so quickly we still had a bit of coffee left. Sean Parnell stood, thanked us, and ushered us out to the lobby.

Wilberforce tossed back the last of his coffee and looked around for a wastebasket. He gave up and plunked the cup down on the nearest unoccupied desk. I waited until we were outside to ask him my burning question:

"Am I a suspect?"

He laughed a rumbling laugh. "Sure you are. Until they've identified someone, everybody's a suspect.

"What you really are is a witness. So far."

He seemed distressingly cheerful about something I considered quite serious. After all, Millicent Pleat and I, while not particularly strong as individuals, might conceivably have ganged up on poor Graham and slung him from the gallows. Anything is possible.

He must have caught my expression, but he brushed it off. "I wouldn't worry about it, Miren," he said. "I've got you covered legally. Just don't strangle anyone for a while, and you'll be fine."

He walked away, his body twitching as he laughed

silently at his own joke. I determined to take him at his word about the worrying. The strangling, I wasn't so sure.

On the way back, I stopped at the library and looked for some nighttime reading. I picked up a mystery set in Venice, and a historical novel about palace intrigue in Constantinople.

When I got home, I saw a manila envelope propped on my mat, leaning against the door. I paused suspiciously for a moment, wondering what tricks some stalker was playing on me now. I bent over to examine it, and relaxed when I saw the message written on the envelope:

Miren,
Just a few ideas...
~Marta

Inside, I dropped the books on the counter and untangled myself from my shoulder bag strap, which had wrapped itself around the handle of a can opener I'd left out, knocking it onto my feet.

I stepped back to the porch and retrieved the envelope. Inside, I found two drawings on cardstock. One showed a floor plan of my re-arranged downstairs.

On the other, Marta had sketched a stylized view of the room, with watercolor washes indicating various hues. My walls were a warm butterscotch, with ivory trim and sea foam green curtains, colors which I never would have thought combined well, but did. She had left my loveseat and Elias' file drawers and had added some lamps and pillows.

As a final touch, curled up on the arm chair, she had added a cat. Camel. Presumably, I had left a window open a crack. I smiled, in spite of myself.

I set the designs aside on my procrastination pile and sat down to check my email.

There was a message from Jodi, asking a few questions about the Caldwell story. And Stephen Melchior had replied.

He was pleased to hear from Elias' kin, and suggested meeting for coffee. There was a Potlatch between Fenton's Crossing and Kingston, and he suggested we meet there. I am not a big fan of overpriced chain coffee, but it seemed acceptable. We agreed on Friday afternoon.

I don't know how he knew me, but he stood up as soon as I walked in the door. He was younger than I expected—tall, sandy haired, and ruggedly handsome in a faintly nerdy way, like so many scientists. He wore metal-rimmed glasses and had a lean, strong-looking body that clearly was the result of hours spent outdoors, and not at the gym. I found myself noticing these attributes in spite of my chosen lifestyle.

"It's the strangest thing," he said, as he sat down with his mocha latte and I with my dark. "Elias had long been interested in a species of the *Lophodermium* fungus that infects conifers. The Agriculture Department has an interest, because it costs timber and ornamental tree growers millions.

"He told me last year that he was observing it at higher and higher altitudes. Apparently it was thriving and expanding its range as global temperatures rose. I put him in touch with Aaron Caldwell, and they were linking their observations.

"He also told me he thought the population he was finding at higher elevations might actually be a new variety of the species, but he wasn't sure. He had me looking at it and enlisted some of the chemists to look under the hood. He was quite sure there was something peculiar about this little beast."

He paused and sipped his brew. A young blond woman sat down at the next table and pulled a laptop out of a large leather shoulder bag. Melchior glanced at her briefly.

"As it happened, this new form of the species was chemically unusual. It contained alkaloids not seen in the varieties we were familiar with. Elias and one of the chemists he worked with were investigating the possibility of finding a pharmaceutical application. We're desperately in need of new forms of antibiotics, as immunity to standard varieties increases. If someone could develop a new class of these drugs, it would have huge implications.

"They're finding very interesting organisms in hostile environments, like acid lakes and open pit mine water," he said. "Fungi and others. And some of them show promise as antibiotics. Here we had an interesting development in an ordinary coniferous forest."

"What happened to the research after my uncle died?" I asked. "Is anyone continuing the project?"

"Well, the chemist he'd been working with died about a month before him. With both of them gone, things have really been in limbo."

We sipped our coffee in silence. I thought about all that knowledge the two men shared, simply evaporating. I thought about the pine needles glued to mounting paper in the drawers of my files. Finally, I spoke.

"I've been wondering what to do with my uncle's laboratory stuff," I said. "I don't need any of the equipment, and I really don't know what to do with the plant specimens he left. After what you've said, I would be reluctant to throw them away."

Melchior almost gasped. "Oh, god. Don't throw anything away!" He had a look of alarm. "Someone should at least go over it before you do anything."

"Well, I was thinking of checking with his department and seeing if they have a use for the specimens. The equipment, to my eye, seems pretty outdated. I had an offer for some of his old instruments from a guy at the university who collects vintage stuff."

Melchior looked up with an odd expression on his face. "May I ask who this collector might be?"

"His name is Lawrence Shaw. Do you know him?" I couldn't think of any reason not to mention his name.

Melchior was silent as he sipped his coffee. He carefully set the cup down on the table and turned it slowly. He took off his glasses and wiped them with the hem of his shirt. "I know him, but not well. His father, Eugene Shaw, was the chemist who was working with your uncle. May I just say that I wouldn't get rid of anything until I've looked at it? Elias didn't have an office at the university, so he kept a lot of things at home."

Was Melchior making a play? I'd have to invite him over to see Uncle Elias' items. Was he trustworthy? How would I know? What did he have against Lawrence? I decided to delay.

"I'd appreciate that. Let me email you when I'm more settled and we can talk about a time."

We got up to leave. Melchior said, "Oh, and one more thing. Have you found anything that looks like a black powder? It would be in a sealed container of some type."

Elias' moldy old shower curtain came to mind, but I shook my head.

"If you do, I'd appreciate it if you'd let me take a look before you do anything. And whatever you do, don't open it. There are things about this organism that we haven't figured out yet."

****

When I pulled into the driveway, I could see an odd-looking gray car pulled up just outside the shrubbery that marked my property line. I recognized it as a Citroën, similar to one a colleague of my father's had driven.

For some reason I really didn't want to park next to someone who seemed to be waiting for me. I backed out of the driveway and parked down at the Star and Garter. I walked back, and the car was still there. A man emerged from the shrubbery, apparently having knocked on my door and given up.

It seemed safer to approach him in this semi-public setting.

"Miss Lassiter?" He approached me with his hand extended. "I'm Lawrence Shaw. I wrote to you about your uncle's possessions."

Like Stephen Melchior, Lawrence was younger than I had expected. He was of medium height with the muscular neck of a wrestler, about my age or a bit younger. He had thick, dark hair and was wearing wraparound sunglasses, which he took off to reveal pale blue eyes that contrasted dramatically with his tan skin. They looked at me with an intensity that was either intriguing or off-putting. I wasn't sure which.

"Oh, hello," I said. "Sorry I didn't get back to you.

I'm still processing things and…" I shrugged.

"Well, I'm sorry to drop by unexpectedly. I was visiting my cousin, Ruth Lovering"—he nodded toward the stone house—"and thought I'd take the opportunity to stop by and introduce myself."

"Oh, you're related to Ruth?" That put me at ease a bit, but not so much that I felt like inviting him into the house.

"Yes, her husband and my father were cousins. I guess you'd say we're cousins by marriage, once removed." He smiled, and his teeth were remarkably white.

I didn't invite him in, but said I appreciated his interest and would let him know when I was ready to do something about the equipment.

He got in his Citroën and drove off. I walked up to the front door and let myself in. I felt a bit foolish about my parking gambit, but the way things were going, it seemed better to be safe than sorry.

Chapter Nineteen

By November, the sun had moved toward the south and no longer woke me streaming in my east window. On the tenth, I awoke to sorrow. It wasn't the season; I had actually found myself savoring the soft-spoken charms of the month. Where earlier, the reddening maples and sumacs were blinding against the impossible blue of the sky, these days the colors had retreated to pewters and rusts, with the purples of feathery fronds and seed pods.

But a dark wing shadowed over me, like a cloud passing before the sun. A darker cloud than most years, because of Seth's visit. Or maybe it was just that my eyelids dropped suddenly. I shook the feeling off, as I did every year, and stepped into the shower for a fresh start.

As I'd expected, a shower and coffee helped restore my balance, and I sat down at my desk with my planner and laptop. I had no interviews or assignments pending, so I thought this might be a good day to move out the remaining boxes of Elias' stuff.

But first, I should tell Ruth about the letters. I waited until a civilized hour, then put on my coat and grabbed the plate she'd sent my cinnamon cookies home on.

Outside, the morning seemed unusually bright. I looked up and realized that most of the leaves had fallen overnight, allowing the sun to reach through the branches and brighten our world. The change in the light from a soft mellow shade to a stark glare was more sudden, and more striking than I recalled back home.

Simeon had moved his huge tractor out of its shed and was attaching something to the back. I suspected it had to do with leaf gathering.

I gave him a wave and slipped across the footbridge and up to Ruth's front door.

She looked happy to see me, as always, and invited me into the kitchen. "Come in, Miren," she said. "Roberta and I are having one of our lively historical debates."

I followed her into the kitchen and set the plate down on the counter. The room was nearly as large as the adjoining keeping room. White metal cabinets, probably from the 1940s, ranged along two walls. A huge electric stove with a side warming cupboard and a drawer for pots occupied most of a third. On a small shelf stood an ornate wooden clock with a short pendulum that clicked briskly. There was an oval braided rug in front of the sink, and a long oak table in the center of the room.

Roberta Jennings sat at the table, stirring a cup of tea. She wore a cranberry colored cardigan over a white blouse, and her glasses were attached to a red cord around her neck. I wondered if she had been a teacher. The glasses sparkled when she looked up from her papers and smiled. She pulled out a chair.

"We're talking about priest holes, Miren," she said. After a moment, she said, "I see your eyes doing a brain Google."

It was true. My eyes had shifted upward and to the left, as I they do when I search my memory for information.

I nodded and settled into the chair she'd offered. Ruth set a cup in front of me and poured hot steamy water from the kettle into the teapot. I began to recite. "Priest holes: spaces hidden in Catholic houses in England in the sixteenth century when saying the Mass was forbidden. Priests would visit families and perform the rites but had to be prepared to hide when royal authorities came sniffing around.

"How did I do?"

"Excellent," Roberta said. "The grand English houses had all sorts of potential hiding places, in attics and ornate stairways. Here in Pennsylvania, on the Underground Railroad, houses like Ruth's sometimes had ingenious trap doors built into stair treads or cupboards, and sometimes into the sides of the large walk-in fireplaces. If you look at Ruth's, you'll see how thick the stone sides are. As you can imagine, it wouldn't be pleasant waiting in there for the bounty hunters to leave."

Roberta picked up a stack of papers and tapped them on the table briskly. "Ruth is convinced her house was a stop, positioned near the river and canal. People would hide in the safe houses, then slip across the river at night. The Philadelphia-New Jersey-New York route ran right through here.

I sipped my tea and asked Roberta if her family was here at the time.

"They sure were," Roberta replied. "Not as passengers, of course—Pennsylvania outlawed slavery in 1780—but they were conductors. My family has been right here since the first census in 1790, and probably earlier. And as freemen, although I don't imagine they started out that way."

I thought about this. "But wasn't this area solidly Quaker?"

"Not solidly; there were quite a few Presbyterians around, mostly because of the Dutch presence. But in the early years in Pennsylvania, quite a few Quakers owned slaves."

That was something I hadn't known. I knew a thing or two about Quakers, mostly from my father, but the idea of their owning other human beings seemed out of kilter.

"Oh, they struggled with that," Ruth said. "They all came around to condemn slavery by the late 1700s. There was plenty of dissension over it. Along with what to do about wars, and all the other things they disagreed about.

"So we're still pursuing my theory that escaped slaves were hidden here," Ruth continued, "and wondered if the same sort of architecture they had in the English houses might have been used.

"Whether or not they knew about priest holes per se," said Roberta, "I'm thinking that's not how escapees were hidden. Often fugitives traveled in groups, even families. They'd be more likely to be hidden in outbuildings."

Roberta had assembled a sheaf of printouts and photocopies. One was an old line drawing of a cupboard whose shelves were hinged and lifted out, as a unit, revealing a small space behind. I remembered Ruth had such a shelf in the next room, near the large fireplace.

I was amused at the thought of two older ladies skulking around the house with a flashlight and tape measure.

"I have a memoir written by my great-grandfather that hints at it," Ruth said. "It talks about his own father, and a somewhat tense discussion he had with a neighbor about the Fugitive Slave Act and what that meant for people here. Some of the people in the area were uncomfortable about breaking the law or having their neighbors do so. I have the feeling that people were hidden on this property, but it would have been kept quiet."

Roberta lifted her cup and drained the last bit. "We're working this from two angles," she told me. "We each have some family records, and other information, from different sides of the story."

They were actually the same side of the story, if from different family histories. The other side of the story would be told by the slave hunters, who no doubt considered themselves repo men doing respectable work recovering stolen property.

For a moment, we were all silent. The clock's pendulum whisked back and forth. Roberta lifted the lid from the teapot and looked inside. She replaced the lid, and I could hear the small scraping sound of two pieces of unglazed pottery coming together.

Something about the ease of Ruth and Roberta's friendship made me wonder how long they had known each other.

"Well, I need to head home," Roberta said, standing and rinsing her cup at the sink. She set it in the drainer, collected her papers, and said her goodbyes.

After she left, I told Ruth I'd found the letters. She

was delighted to hear it and said I might want to consider renting a safe deposit box for their safekeeping.

We chatted for a bit, and as I turned to go, I said, "Oh, and I met your cousin, Lawrence."

"Ah, yes. Lawrence." She had a faintly chagrined tone, as if Lawrence might have been a handful in his day.

****

Lawrence and I had exchanged phone numbers in our emails, and the next morning, he called. He said he was in the neighborhood and would be happy to drop by if I was ready. I don't like being pressured, and his interest was beginning to feel a bit like pressure.

I told him I was heading out the door to get my car inspection, and maybe another time would be better.

"Why don't I pick you up after you drop it off, and we can find some decent coffee and talk? It'll be better than waiting room stuff. I can stop by to look at your items some other time."

For a split second I thought about reasons to say no but concluded that coffee was safe. I told him I'd be waiting in front of Wurtz's Gas and Garage at eleven.

I was early, so I checked my car in, handed over my registration and insurance cards, and told the clerk about a rattle in the front right side. I considered sitting in the cramped waiting room, but someone had raised the volume on a television broadcast about a celebrity who either was or wasn't pregnant. The set was garishly red and blue, and the anchors grinned like well-coiffed sharks. A breathless subtitle about some kind of scandal ran across the bottom of the screen.

I beat a hasty retreat and stood waiting outside,

savoring the gas and oil smells and listening to the clanking and buzzing of auto repair equipment. Lawrence pulled up in the Citroën. I got in, and he asked if I had a preference in coffee shops.

I didn't, really, so I tossed out Potlatch as a suggestion. He responded with silence. I glanced over, puzzled, and sensed an eyeroll behind his dark glasses. Presumably, his contempt for overpriced, over-hip chain coffee went without saying. Still, his tone was polite when he suggested Krakatoa House of Java, up the river in Cooperville.

He drove silently, which was fine with me. I was a little uncomfortable riding in a car with someone I knew nothing about, except that he seemed to set Stephen Melchior on edge.

Since I don't spend a lot of money or attention on coffee shop coffee, I'd never been to Krakatoa. I had to concede, though, that it had a pleasant atmosphere. Tribal textiles. Batiks. Lots of plants vining all over. It offered wet grind coffee from exquisite beans undoubtedly hand plucked by unionized bean pickers with pensions and dental plans.

There was no line. Lawrence ordered a chai latte, and I requested my usual black. We chose a small wooden table near the window. He slipped out of his corduroy blazer. He was wearing a charcoal Henley T-shirt. His shoulders sloped down from that thick, muscular neck.

It occurred to me, a bit too late, that this was sort of a date. People often start the process with daytime coffee, and I wondered what Lawrence was thinking about the situation.

But he began with science.

"My father and your uncle were colleagues," he said. "They both worked on different ends of the same problem in plant pathology, or in your uncle's case, fungal pathology. My father had great respect for your uncle.

"But he died last summer. He had a massive stroke."

"I'm sorry," I said. "That must have been hard for you."

Lawrence stared down at his cup. "It was. And then your uncle died. It was a loss to science. They were really making progress on the project. They leave a lot of unfinished business behind."

The subject turned to Elias' scientific equipment, and I was vague about what I had. I preferred to hear what he wanted. He was almost as vague and turned the conversation to his work.

He said he taught general science to middle school students and enjoyed getting the kids involved by setting up complicated equipment and experiments. "They like the mad scientist look of the glassware and tubes and puffs of smoke," he said, "even though that's not seen much in modern labs."

I hadn't realized he was a teacher. I had gotten the impression he worked at the university. I shifted away from that topic.

"So Ruth Lovering is your relative? Did you grow up near Fenton's Crossing?"

Lawrence shook his head. He told me about his childhood in New Jersey, and I told him as little as possible about my past.

He took a sip of latte. "Did your uncle ever tell you how he discovered the fungus was toxic?"

"Toxic to people?" I was somewhat taken aback. Melchior hadn't said anything about toxicity; he just said it was a bit mysterious.

"No," I said. "I really knew very little about his work."

"Well, he was collecting *Lophodermium* on pine needles somewhere in Nevada and found what he thought was a dead chipmunk lying beside his collecting pack. It had chewed its way through the canvas, although why it would bother with that particular stash, it's hard to imagine. It's not as if there weren't plenty of pine needles around.

"He was curious, so he put the chipmunk in a metal box and checked it a few hours later. It was hopping around, good as new.

"That intrigued him, and when he got back, he had my father analyze the material chemically."

Lawrence paused, perhaps for effect. He liked to keep his audience in suspense.

I obliged.

"What did he find out?"

"In its unpurified state, the fungus resembled certain compounds that suppress the central nervous system. But when my father purified it, it showed promise as an antibiotic. As you can imagine, a new class of effective antibiotic would be very valuable. They began to collaborate on an effort to interest a pharmaceutical company in conducting research."

I thought about that for a while. "And now they're both dead."

"Yes. They're both dead. I don't know if your uncle's colleagues have plans to pursue this route or not, but it's a shame it's been disrupted."

He lifted his cup to his mouth but held it there, not drinking. He seemed lost in thought.

His muscular physique reminded me of Jason, a high school classmate who was on the wrestling team. I hadn't thought of him in a very long time. We didn't really date; most kids then just hung around together in a loose-knit group. But he'd show up at the *Marmot* office to help out when I was busy putting an issue to bed, and I attended a few of his wrestling matches.

He was a good person, funny and practical. On several occasions, we held hands. Twice, we kissed.

And then my father died, and that was that.

I hadn't realized how long we'd been there until the sunlight slid out from behind a building across the street and caused me to squint.

The couple at the next table were taking cell phone pictures of each other. I got the sense that they were lovers of some sort, maybe newlyweds.

The man reached into a backpack and took out a proper camera. He fiddled with some controls and focused on the woman. There was a sudden flash, and Lawrence gasped and started. He grabbed his sunglasses and slipped them on.

"I can't be without these," he said, "especially when driving. I have optical epilepsy. I take medication for it. But I need these in bright light and glare."

Great. Another topic to take to my friend Google. Was it was safe to drive with Lawrence? I changed the subject back to the university department and our scientific relatives. The name of Stephen Melchior came up.

"Oh, you've talked to Steve Melchior?" He had an odd expression—much like Melchior's when I mentioned Lawrence. What was going on between these guys?

Lawrence seemed about to say more when someone at a window table got up and left, and the sun, no longer blocked, streamed directly into my face. Lawrence looked intently at me. He removed his sunglasses and asked, "What color are your eyes?"

I shifted in my seat to move out of the sun. Generally, when men ask me about my eyes, it's a sign to change the subject.

"Light brown, I guess."

He stared for a moment. His own face was in shadow, but his eyes stood out like blue flames.

"Quince jelly," he said, and nodded in satisfaction. He checked his watch. "You want to call and see if your car is ready?"

"You can drop me back any time," I said. "It should be done, but if it's not, it won't be a long wait."

We got up to leave, and he reached for his sunglasses.

Quince jelly?

Chapter Twenty

The temperatures grew cooler, but the water in the river hadn't gotten the message. The cold air and still-warm water conjured up fog, which lay on the surface like a down comforter and obscured the current.

Wednesday morning, I brought my coffee upstairs and watched the foggy river from my east window.

Suddenly a shadowy figure emerged from the mist. A man stood on the bank, apparently trying to see the other side through the fog.

I couldn't see him clearly, but I could tell he was wearing a blue coat, tan leggings, and a tri-cornered hat. He was carrying what looked like a musket, and picked his way slowly along the bank, watching the other side.

I closed my eyes briefly in disbelief. When I opened them again, the figure was still there, watching the river.

Was I looking at Eliphalet Fenton himself? An apparition? A re-enactor involved in a dress rehearsal? I thought about going down there to see who he was, but I wasn't dressed and I figured he was harmless anyway, as long as I stayed out of musket range. I would have to ask one of the village elders who or what he was.

As I watched, he moved along the riverbank away from me, and soon was obscured by the Butterfields' house. Shortly after, he emerged on the road, and I watched him from the front window as he headed across the end of our driveway and out of sight. I got a closer look at the firearm, which proved not to be a musket at all, but an ordinary modern deer rifle.

This was the day Stephen Melchior was coming to look at Elias' possessions. I'd given him directions, but when the time approached I waited outside in case he had trouble finding the house. The hedge was bare now, and as I examined the branches and thought about pruning them back a bit, Simeon approached from behind his cottage.

"Morning, Miren. What's up?

"Hi, Simeon. I'm waiting for a guy who wants to look at some of my uncle's scientific stuff."

"Ah. Someone you know?"

"Well, not well. He's a Kingston professor, and I have spoken with him before." I paused. "That okay with you?"

"Well, now. Not my business, but just know that I'm here, should you need me."

He turned and started back to his house. I honestly could not figure him out. He was unassuming and quiet, but seemed a bit over-interested in my well-being.

At that point, a dark green Subaru hatchback pulled in and headed our way across the gravel.

It pulled up to the hedge, and Melchior got out. He greeted me and opened the back hatch and took out a satchel that resembled a doctor's medical bag.

"Well-hidden spot you have here," he said, surveying the scene. "I must have been down the highway a dozen times, and never knew this was here."

As we went inside, I gave him the thirty-second history of Fenton's Crossing and how it got lost in time.

Melchior put the bag down and shrugged out of his

tan barn coat. I hung it on the coat rack. He refused my offer of coffee and went straight to work.

I showed him the instruments I'd left on the shelf and pointed out the collecting books. I indicated the specimen drawers.

I sat down with my laptop and checked my email while he examined everything. Melchior worked in silence for some time. Finally, he closed the top specimen drawer and asked, "Do you know why Elias kept these?"

"No," I said. "Maybe he kept his favorites? Especially rare ones?"

"Well, we can check that in his accession books. In the field, they record everything they collect and indicate dates, descriptions, and locations. They do a preliminary species identification, although that sometimes changes when they get back to the lab and I take a look.

"I'll check with Mia Sung at the department herbarium and see whether they could use any of these. Most of them are quite common, so I'm just wondering why he kept them."

"Dr. Melchior, I don't need them. I'd rather have them put to use, but if not, they'll go in the trash."

He stepped back, startled. "Oh, not yet! Not yet!"

After a moment, he said, "And I'd actually prefer it if you'd call me Stephen. Most people do."

He looked up at the shelved notebooks. "Can I take some of these with me? I'll give you a receipt."

I didn't feel the need for formalities, but he was already scrutinizing the dates on the accession books and writing in his notebook.

"The instruments can go, if you don't want them,"

he said. "But I'd hang on to the specimens a bit longer. Don't get rid of them until you hear from me, okay?" he said, tearing out a page and handing it to me. "I won't take any today but may want a few after checking with Mia."

He packed the notebooks in his satchel and looked around for his coat. I handed it to him, then escorted him out to his car.

As he drove away, Simeon emerged from his front door, waved, and retreated inside.

So Simeon had kept watch. Did I like that? Was he being protective in a neighborly way, or was he being a bit of a snoop? What if Stephen was my lover? Would I want Simeon lurking around, waiting for him to leave?

Chapter Twenty-One

Holidays pose a difficulty for solitude junkies like me. I don't mind spending them alone—I actually enjoy a day off to enjoy a turkey sandwich, a few glasses of wine, and a novel I'd never had the time to dig down into. But other people feel compelled to invite us loners to their holiday festivities.

This year, I actually welcomed Jodi's invitation. Without a regular job, I didn't really need a day off. And I had a lot on my mind. I didn't relish the idea of spending the day alone, brooding about Seth and how his visit had thrown me off balance.

So I agreed to join a group of newsroom orphans for turkey. Jodi and her husband Greg lived in an expanded Levittown house, which meant that the original carport had been converted into a family room and an upstairs addition provided more bedrooms for a growing family.

On the Tuesday before Thanksgiving, I headed for the store to pick up cherries and cream cheese and other ingredients for my specialty. I was loading my grocery bags into the Corolla when I heard my name.

I turned, and there was Roberta Jennings coming toward me, carrying her own modest purchases in a reusable fabric bag.

"How are you getting on, Miren?"

I closed the trunk. "I'm managing well, thanks.

And how are you and Ruth progressing with your historical research?"

"Oh, we haven't found the smoking gun. But we've assembled some fine details about this area that nobody's really written about before." She looked wistful for a moment.

"I have great admiration for writers," she said, shifting the bag from one hand to the other. "I'd love to write up the project myself, but I find it just about impossible to get started."

I nodded sympathetically.

"I shouldn't have so much trouble," she said. "I taught school for more than thirty years. I know my grammar. It just isn't a natural thing for me, and I admire reporters who can produce readable material on a daily basis."

"It's often hard for people like teachers and editors," I said, congratulating myself on my earlier assessment of her occupation. "You're probably looking over your own shoulder, grading your work as you go. The trick is to let yourself write badly at the beginning, and not worry about perfection."

I hoped—perhaps uncharitably—that she wouldn't ask me to help. If there's one thing I dread, it's being asked to read and critique someone's writing. In a professional setting, I'm happy to offer suggestions, but most lay people are terribly emotionally involved in what they've written and are usually seeking praise rather than useful suggestions.

But Roberta didn't stray into that territory. She told me about the research she and Ruth had done, and said she was also considering writing a family genealogy or memoir. I thought that would be fascinating. And I said so.

"Paul Butterfield told me about a course in memoir writing at the community college, and I've been thinking about signing up," she said. "That would get me moving."

"Exactly," I said. "You'll have to write regularly. There's nothing like regular assignments and deadlines to keep you on track."

I envisioned Roberta at her desk, poring over old family letters. I suddenly remembered the old botanical letters hidden in Elias' stationery drawer.

"By the way, do you know anything about where to go to have historic documents authenticated and appraised?" I asked. "I came across some things that I might want to sell, but I'm not sure of their value."

Roberta looked thoughtful for a moment. Then she said, "Well, I'm more interested in what old documents say, rather than their value. But if I were you, I'd take them to New Hope and check with someone at Brimstoke and Associates. They've been around for years and should give you a straight answer."

I thanked her, then remembered another question. I told her about the apparition I'd seen in the fog, by the river bank.

"Do you know who that might have been," I asked. "He looked like a Revolutionary War soldier, complete with musket."

Roberta smiled. "Oh, that has to be Jim Bollinger. He's quite fanatic about re-enacting the war. You say he was by himself? Scouting the river?"

"It looked that way," I said, and Roberta nodded.

"Jim has wanted to re-enact Eliphalet Fenton's crossing of the Delaware for years, and he tries to get the Christmas Crossing board to include it as part of the regular re-enactment. He's never gotten much of a hearing, and I believe he harbors quite a bit of resentment."

I had more questions for Roberta, about her writing projects and her teaching career and her family's centuries in this place. But I glanced at her grocery bags, still in her hands. "Your ice cream must be melting, Roberta. I shouldn't keep you. Thanks for your information, and I do think the memoir class is a great idea."

On the drive home, an evil thought flashed into my head: I'd told Roberta that I'd come across old documents that might have value. What if Roberta—mild-mannered, bookish Roberta—was my burglar? Stranger things have happened.

On Thanksgiving morning, I baked my gâteau Basque and packed it for the trip. Dinner was planned for early evening, timed to begin when the football game ended.

I took the back roads. Most of the cornfields had been scalped to stubble, but one was still being harvested. A combine moved through the field, paired with a massive open truck. As the contraption progressed, it sucked up the stalks, separated the dried kernels from the ears, and sprayed them in a golden arc into the truck. Clearly, it would take several trucks to accommodate one field's bounty.

After Rogers Brothers produce stand, with its heaps of pumpkins, gourds and Indian corn, the road straightened out. It ran through a stand of maples, newly bare, and standing tall and straight. The sun, more horizontal these days, cast a harsh, striped shadow across the road and into the side of my eyes, as if I were going past a supermarket barcode scanner.

I squeezed the Corolla into a space a few doors down, and schlepped my covered cake pan up to the door. The oldest of the four kids answered.

"Hi, Ryan. Hope I'm not late." A cloud of evocative scents enveloped me.

"It's okay," he said, closing the door behind me. "We won't eat until the game's over. What's in there?"

He craned toward my dish. He was eleven, if I remembered correctly, with that ungainly quality boys get when they're about to burst into adolescence.

"It's a cake. Sort of a flat pie-shaped thing, with cherries. You'll like it."

"As long as it's not more sweet potatoes," he said, with a shudder.

Jodi had the oven door open, checking the turkey. She straightened and lifted the lid on my pan.

"Ooh! It's that awesome cake! It doesn't need the fridge, does it?"

"Nope. Anywhere's fine. On the table?"

"No." Jodi looked distracted and started to move things around on the counter. "All that stuff has to go over here so we can set up the kids' table.

"We have the usual stuffing and mashed potatoes for gravy soakage, and Jen's bringing sweet potatoes with marshmallows. Tradition!"

There was a chorus of baritone cheers from the den.

I glanced around the corner into the den, where Pradip and Ezra were high-fiving, and Spencer and Greg looked downcast.

Greg shook his head and came into the kitchen,

heading for the fridge.

"Score is twenty-four to seven, overtime unlikely." He grabbed a handful of longnecks. "Everything okay? Need some hands?"

"It's fine, sweetie," Jodi said. "Your hands will get their chance after dinner."

Greg left, and she turned to me. "So. Probably forty-five minutes or less until turkey time, preceded by gravy, the warming of various things, kid table set-up. About fifteen minutes for you to bring me up to date. Wine?"

She grabbed two glasses and poured us each some Riesling out of a jug.

We leaned against the counters and caught up. I liked Jodi's house; it had a practical layout, on a slab like all its neighbors, with the open, optimistic look of the 1950s. It was nicely decorated, but it had that scuffed look of a house with a lot of children.

I told her about Fenton's Crossing, about coping with reduced income, trying to unravel the mysteries of my uncle's research and possessions. I did not tell her about Seth.

She nodded thoughtfully. "I'll give you as much work as I can, but naturally, after laying off my feature writer, now they've slashed the freelance budget.

"But it's not all bad!! We editors aren't editors any more. "We're now"—her expression conveyed an expectant drum roll—"content coaches!"

"Content coaches? Good lord! Why? And why would they eliminate features? Those are the best-read stories in the paper!"

"They just want everything for nothing. The plan is to have beat reporters write features for me when they 'have time.' " She made air quotes, causing the Riesling to slosh precariously in her glass.

"Hmph," I said. "When will they ever 'have time'? Plus, reporters aren't interchangeable. Can you imagine Spencer trying to write a heart-warming human interest story?"

The doorbell rang and I opened it to let Jen in. "Hi, Miren? Happy Thanksgiving!"

"Hi, Jen. Everything okay at the paper?" I held the pan of sweet potatoes while she took off her coat.

"Oh, sure! People keep dying, so I guess I'm pretty safe!" She added a toothy smile and an anxious little nod, as she did to every statement, as if to say, "Did I do okay?"

Jodi greeted her and took the pan. Jen offered to help, but Jodi sent her into the den with a beer; Jen was a known sports fan with a particular interest in Ezra.

Thundering feet came down the stairs. It was Laura, their youngest.

"Mommy, when's dinner?"

"Soon, honey. Go tell Clarissa and Matt to wash their hands and come down."

I cleared the kitchen table and set out paper plates and plastic glasses for four. Jody turned off the oven and dragged the roaster from the oven. I waited a few minutes before sliding the side dishes in to warm. Jodi drained drippings and began the gravy process.

Jodi told the kids to go sit with their dad while we got things ready. It wasn't long before extended cheers and laughter from the den signaled the end of the game, and everyone trooped into the kitchen

The kids were ordered to sit down at the kitchen table. I watched with pleasure as they scrambled onto their customary chairs, knowing where they belonged, clicking into place like parts of a puzzle, moving from chaos to order, like leaves falling up to their places on the tree.

We grownups needed to be assigned our seats in the dining room, and Greg poured wine as Ezra and I brought side dishes in and set them down on trivets. Jodi had set aside portions of each dish for the kids and served them at the kitchen table.

Finally, everyone was seated, and Jodi lit the candles. Greg bowed his head and said, "Bless these gifts to our use and us to loving service, and what we desire for ourselves may we desire for others."

We passed bowls of potatoes, both regular and sweet, and stuffing. Platters of carrots, green beans and sliced turkey made their way around the table.

We toasted the *Clarion* and its diminished status and dug into our meals. There was some discussion of the football game that just ended. I learned that the paper's top management had spent a fortune on a re-design, handled by the brother-in-law of one of the vice presidents. It would perk up the section fronts, supposedly to make the *Clarion* look fresh and contemporary. Jodi dreaded its implementation; it would shrink the news hole and confuse readers.

"Fur will fly," she said, and heaved a long sigh.

Spencer updated us on the Farnsworth investigation, which was going nowhere, and the conversation turned to Mark, who was celebrating the holiday with his own family. Pradip said he thought Mark was getting ready to publish, an event everybody knew was imminent when he clammed up, and when Abraham Wilberforce went into F.X.'s office and slammed the door behind him.

Jodi, who, as an editor, was probably in on Mark's project, said little. Those who knew less were eager to share their knowledge.

"It has to do with the Wintergreen estate," Spencer said. "There's a lot of activity over there, after what, fifteen years of nothing? Every once in a while, you see bulldozers clearing trees, but nothing ever comes of it."

"How can anyone tell?" Ezra asked "The place is so overgrown it's just about invisible."

"Oh, you can see, especially if you take some of those little streets behind the property. Kids play there all the time. They're probably not supposed to, but they do anyway."

The Wintergreen tract was about ten acres of dense woods, in the center of which was the shell of a grand stone house built in the eighteenth century. Something was going on there, but Mark was being unusually quiet about it.

Everyone had run out of speculation, apparently. Jen changed the subject.

"Does anyone know how F.X. was given that name? Francis Xavier is, you know…"

"Oh," said Jodi. "Back when his parents got married, it was pretty unusual for Catholics and Jews to marry. Apparently his parents were fine with working out the details in their marriage, but the grandparents were fit to be tied."

Jodi held the plate of turkey out, soliciting requests for thirds. No one accepted.

"So his mother's family had to bite their tongue when their sweet little Irish daughter became Mrs. Rosenzweig," she continued. "His father's family grumbled that their nice Jewish boy was married by a priest. They went on and on, until the first grandson was born. Their nice Jewish boy now had a son named Francis Xavier, but everyone stopped fussing and started doting on him."

As the meal wound down, giggles from the kids' table merged with the hum of adult conversation, all punctuated by the pop of an occasional wine bottle being uncorked.

Then pies were brought out—my gâteau Basque joined Spencer's pumpkin, and both received rapturous compliments.

Soon, Greg fired up the coffee pot so people could detox a bit before driving home. Jodi distributed pans and platters, freshly washed, to those who had brought them. Spencer held my pie plate while I slipped on my coat. As he handed it to me, he said, "I didn't want to share this with the multitude, but I wanted to let you know off the record that they found some odd clues in the museum."

I thought of that orange windbreaker and the man hurrying out of the museum before anyone knew what had happened.

Spencer was still talking.

"They're still looking for a motive. Their initial search revealed one exhibit that showed signs of tampering. There's a crack in the glass that the custodial crew noticed the day of the murder, but thought was probably accidental. And not only that, it looks as though the door that provides access to the exhibit was picked, or an attempt was made."

Lock picking?

I gulped. Then I got my voice back. I asked, "What

exhibit was that?"

"They said it was the one with old-fashioned medical equipment—saws, tongs, things you wouldn't want anywhere near you. Creepy stuff. Scientific doodads."

Chapter Twenty-Two

I was on the third rung of the ladder, with a paint tray of Chestnut Soufflé and a roller. I'd cleaned the walls, spackled the holes, and spread a drop cloth over everything. I was making my house look—with a few exceptions—like Marta's vision.

I'd studied her arrangement and marveled at how a simple switch of elements—tables, couches—made a difference, both visually and in terms of comfort. Instead of trying to line up furniture against walls, Marta had centered my seating area in the room, over an area rug. I replaced Elias' wooden table with his old footlocker and covered it with a colorful rug; that gave me both a coffee table and storage. I'd made a note to myself to buy some kind of floor lamp for behind the couch, where there was no room for a table.

I'd resisted Marta's insights at first. But as I moved furniture around, Elias' house changed into a home. I found myself studying her color schemes and shopping for paint.

My previous dwelling places were humble and rented. I'd never really had a place of my own that felt like a home. And it was growing on me.

As four o'clock approached, I could sense the light diminishing, and I cleaned my painting supplies. After what seemed like hours staring at walls, I needed a view. Upstairs, I watched the river for a few minutes out my east window.

My southern view, over the loft railing and out the high windows, revealed a trick of November light I'd noticed in Nevada. Pewter clouds formed a ceiling in the darkening sky, and as the sun angled toward the horizon, it suddenly slipped beneath the cloud cover and shot horizontal shafts of gold across the landscape. The light, and accompanying shadows, extended eastward, flat and uninterrupted. If I'd been able to crane out my window and look left, I'd see windows in New Jersey flaring with reflected brilliance.

Downstairs, I took another look at the remaining piles and boxes. I'd been moving things from side to side as I painted, and it wasn't practical to keep them around if I was trying to make the place look nice. Without a basement or attic, I couldn't really keep stuff I didn't need. At least I could get rid of the scientific equipment. It was time to tell Lawrence he could take what he wanted.

I sent him an email and called it a day. I poured my usual white wine, and anticipated my new, uncluttered space.

My laptop pinged, and I checked my email. Lawrence had responded; we agreed on Thursday for him to come by and collect the microscopes, the scale, several boxes of flasks and other glassware, and assorted smaller items.

****

I had a momentary pang of unease as I thought about Lawrence in my house—for what reason, I couldn't imagine. I thought wryly that if anything untoward happened, Simeon would be sure to save me.

Lawrence arrived with the trunk of his car full of

cartons and old newspapers (the *Clarion*, I was happy to observe). I'd placed the items on a table, and I stood watching Lawrence as he examined them. His gaze kept wandering, noting the built-in cupboards under the stairs and the loft railing above.

Finally, he suggested a price, which seemed reasonable to me, and began packing his purchases.

After he'd loaded the trunk, he came back in, holding a checkbook. He asked about the map drawer. "It's a useful piece," he said. "It's not relevant to my collection, but I could use it if you don't want it."

I declined; it was still full of maps and items I hadn't looked at closely, since my first look at the maps had made me uneasy. I needed to take a closer look. I did, however, ask if he had any interest in the drying oven. I admitted I didn't even know if it worked.

He walked back into the kitchen and took a look. He picked up the old electrical cord and examined the plug.

"Wow, that's pretty old," he said. "Not exactly antique, though. Sure you can't use it? You could bake a pizza in it."

"I think not," I said. "I don't want to think what else has been in there."

"Oh, why not? I'll find a use for it." He suggested a price and wrote a check for the total.

Lawrence suggested we consummate our transaction with another stop at Krakatoa. I couldn't think of a reason not to, so I got into the Citroën and we headed for Cooperville.

He ordered the chai masala. I ordered my usual, and we took our usual table near the window.

"So, did you grow up in Nevada?" He pronounced

the first "a" to rhyme with "ah," in the Spanish manner that outsiders sometimes use. I gave him the edited version of my past and didn't bother to correct his pronunciation. I had the feeling Lawrence didn't like being corrected, but the next time I used the word, I said it correctly—with the "a" rhyming with "hat."

I could sense a flicker of resentment in him. I wondered if the man had any sense of humility at all, or even whimsy.

I always find it odd when very intelligent people are humorless. To me, humor and wit emerge from a lively, inventive mind, and it's hard to imagine someone being lively and inventive without having some fun along the way. I understand people being serious and devoted to their work, but so much of what one might call genius derives from a playful mind.

Even in a short sample, like a comment on a blog, you can sense a person's depth of thinking. Some people leave so much unsaid, implied; they're showing the tip of a fascinating iceberg, leaving plenty in reserve. More ordinary minds laboriously present their best stuff.

I turned my attention back to Lawrence. "I was in gifted classes," he was saying, "but hated being forced to do stuff that didn't interest me. It's not unusual for gifted kids to have trouble completing assignments, paying attention, and such. That's one reason I enjoy teaching. I try to convey that there are certain things they have to do, but I can understand what's giving them trouble.

"My parents may have been overly protective of me, because of the seizures. But once they were able to control my condition with medication and environmental management, like these"—he lifted the dark glasses from the table—"they seemed to switch over to a new obsession: my IQ."

Lawrence was recounting how he'd been tested and retested and enrolled in gifted classes and enrichment camps, when the small temple bells attached to the front door clanked. I looked up to see Spencer and Mark walk in. They didn't actually walk; Mark loped and Spencer bounced. They didn't notice me at first; their eyes went immediately to the menu posted on the wall behind the counter. It gave me a moment to marvel at their differences—Mark over six feet tall, with crisp auburn hair and a shabby car coat; Spencer barely five-seven, with neatly combed, dark blond hair and a navy pea jacket over a light blue cotton sweater.

"Two of my colleagues just came in," I told Lawrence. He twisted around to get a look.

"The tall guy and the short guy?"

"Right. The police reporter and our investigative reporter."

I greeted them as they passed us after placing their orders. Mark had a file folder under his arm, so I assumed they were collaborating on something. They nodded but didn't stop.

Lawrence kept glancing over toward them, so when we were ready to leave, I walked over to their table and introduced them.

"We're tracking down assorted evildoers," Mark said, whacking the file. "I think we'll have something within a few weeks."

Spencer nodded.

Just then, the barista called out Mark's name. He had opened the file and was busy fumbling with papers, so Spencer jumped up and went to the bar.

We said goodbye as Spencer sat down with Mark's cup, and left Krakatoa. The bells jingled behind us. Lawrence seemed unnerved by the brief conversation. I was about to make some sort of wisecrack but reconsidered. Lawrence wasn't an easy person to banter with.

Back in his car, I asked him about his scientific background. Had he worked in a lab? Did he have a degree in science, or education?

"Actually," he said, "I was in a PhD. program in biochemistry at Rutgers, but my advisor turned out to be an idiot. I left with a master's degree, which isn't good for much beyond working as a lab tech. Teaching had more appeal for me."

It wasn't that late, but the light was fading as Lawrence drove me home. We said little during the trip. I wondered what his intentions were. I wondered if he was in a relationship, gay or straight. So far, he'd said nothing that pushed our relationship beyond a polite business arrangement, which was fine with me.

****

My sleep ritual was malfunctioning. The bad thoughts crept out from the shadowy edge of the clearing and were moving into the light where I couldn't ignore them.

The IMAX screen refused to provide the swirls and flickers that morphed into dreams. Instead, it remained gray. And cold. And dead.

During my weary waking hours, I wondered what to do about Seth.

Was he going to show up on my doorstep every day, like an abandoned kitten? In some ways that's what he was, with his mother dead or long gone, and his father in prison. But why was he my responsibility, just because of a few coincidences about birthdays and the like? I didn't want a mother-son relationship, and I really didn't want one with someone who wasn't even my son.

I had looked forward to moving into the cottage of a reclusive elderly man, expecting to live my own reclusive life. But here I was, bombarded with jolly neighbors, not to mention editors and interviewees, and now a Lost Boy who had somehow imprinted on me.

Clearly, I was going to have to get to the bottom of this.

Did Seth have a birth certificate? Had he ever heard from either of his aunts? Because the only way to resolve this was to find out who his mother was, once and for all. She may well have died at the compound. But whoever she was, she wasn't me. And I needed to make him understand that.

Chapter Twenty-Three

Christmas dawned cold and hard, with a dusting of snow like cinders. Ruth Lovering had invited me to have Christmas dinner with her, and the idea actually appealed to me. I imagined a yule log in that enormous fireplace, and holly garlands draped around the ancient house. But I'd had enough togetherness at Thanksgiving to last the season, so I declined.

I put on some Christmas music and assembled my solitary luncheon of baked salmon with dill, new potatoes, asparagus, and several chocolate truffles for dessert. A splash (or two) of Prosecco added to the holiday mood.

Afterward, I drove into the village of Washington Crossing for the annual re-enactment of the crossing of the Delaware. I found a parking place behind the post office and walked toward the embarkation point near the visitors' center. Crowds of families, all bundled up against the cold, headed for the river. Musket shots rang out as we approached.

From a distance, I could see the stone façade of the Ferry Inn—quite different from the one in Fenton's Crossing—where Washington had dined before launching his daring night-time crossing.

The crowd milled around the smaller stone buildings. A woman in a long skirt and cloak, her hair covered with a white bonnet, sat at a table dispensing hot cider and pamphlets about the park and the foundation that sponsored the crossing. An enormous white barn loomed right next to the river; it was home to the forty-foot Durham boats until they're hauled out each December.

At the appointed time, an aide marched to the door of the Inn and rapped ceremoniously.

The door opened, and George himself marched out, accompanied by his top generals, to cheers and applause from the audience.

He addressed the crowd, in character, and then unrolled a scroll. It was Thomas Paine's "Sunshine Patriot" speech.

"These are the times that try men's souls…The summer soldier and the sunshine patriot will, in this crisis, shrink from the service of their country; but he that stands it now, deserves the love and thanks of man and woman…"

I watched the river as he began, and as I listened, I shifted my gaze to the men in uniform, lined up, standing at attention. I thought of what it must have been like, near midnight on a bitter cold Christmas, loading onto the black Durham boats, crossing the dark river, struggling up the icy bank, marching many miles and then into uncertain battle.

There were more musket shots and drums, signaling it was time for the company to march down to the river and step into the three replica boats. The oarsmen were awkward, not nearly as skilled as John Glover's original regiment from Marblehead, Mass. But they pushed off bravely, heading toward the other shore, where another crowd greeted Washington with cheers and applause when he stepped ashore.

After a brief ceremony on the Jersey side, everyone formed up and marched back across the narrow bridge. In the crowd I spotted a familiar uniform I'd seen in the fog a few weeks ago. I waved. Jim Bollinger saw me and nodded slightly but did not break character.

Chapter Twenty-Four

All my months have colors, so on New Year's Eve I was watching red December shift into light blue January. My colored months form a circular year. I stand in the center and watch as the winter months march toward the equinox, round the curve into summer, and on through the year, turning like the rim of a wheel with me at its hub.

I don't often go to New Year's parties, but when I do, I take care to avoid the mistletoe. I would have to either leave before midnight, or conveniently disappear into the bathroom during the countdown to avoid being grabbed and kissed.

Marta had told me that several of the Fenton's Crossing folk would be gathering at the Star and Garter to ring in the New Year. I responded vaguely, thinking I'd be happier staying home with a glass of wine and a good book. Maybe I'd stream Times Square on the laptop.

But on the 31st, I reconsidered. I felt just restless enough that a quiet evening at home didn't appeal as much as it often did. I slipped into a pair of black pants and my new (or old) shimmery amber blouse. Or was it quince jelly?

At nine thirty, I put some cash and my keys into a small shoulder bag, got into my coat and headed on foot toward the Star and Garter.

I was surprised to find the party in full swing. Jim Bollinger, not in uniform except for a festive tricorn hat, was in animated conversation with Roberta Jennings, who was wearing a bright seasonal sweater with holly leaves knitted into it. On closer inspection, I realized that Jim was being more than animated; he was red-faced, whether from holiday beverages or anger, I couldn't tell, and moving closer to Roberta. She stood her ground and looked admirably calm.

I took off my coat and did a quick mistletoe inspection. I detected a good-sized bunch hanging over the far end of the bar and determined to avoid the area. I heard my name and turned to find Simeon smiling broadly. He had tied his gray hair back with a glittery elastic band such as pre-teen girls wear. He stood next to a giant of a man, heavily bearded, and with sinister looking tattoos crawling out from a vest he wore without a shirt.

I waved to Simeon and squeezed through the crowd toward the bar, eager for a glass of wine.

"Miren!" Desmond said. "Welcome, and Happy New Year to you!"

He wore a bright green sweater and the satisfied look of a publican welcoming a robust crowd.

"And the same to you." I ordered my wine and glanced around the room. "This is quite a group. It's nice to see the Crossing folk have turned out."

"It is. And I took an advert out in that paper you used to work for. Apparently it's well-read!"

I took my wine and slipped him a twenty. When he handed me my change, I popped some into the tip jar.

Just then Marta came up the stairs, carrying a six-pack of Pabst Blue Ribbon. She set it on the bar in front of Desmond, who made a face before storing the bottles in an under-counter refrigerator.

Marta surprised me on two counts. First, she had departed from her usual earthy fiber wardrobe, and had opted for a shiny silver blouse and sparkly earrings. And it surprised me that she was helping Desmond out, as if she were an employee and not a customer. Or maybe as if she were a close friend. I pondered the implications.

She turned and saw me. "Hi, Miren! Gee, you look great!"

"You too, Marta. We're both sort of metallic tonight."

She eyed my attire. "You're either metallic, or maybe botanical. Or maybe honey? Molasses?"

"Whatever it is, it's shiny and seasonal," I said. "So, you're helping out tonight?"

"Just until Desmond's new guy arrives. He says business is picking up and he could use an extra pair of hands, so he has this kid coming in part time. I'm just pitching in for now."

I left her to her helpful activities and checked in with Simeon. He smiled broadly and introduced me, quite properly, to his friend. "Miren, this is Leo Slaughter. Leo, Miren Lassiter, my neighbor."

"Hello, Leo." I said. "Happy New Year."

He raised his bottle of Budweiser and nodded but didn't speak.

"So, Miren. Got any resolutions lined up? Leo and I have been working on ours. We're going to be more perfect dudes in the coming year."

"I don't see how that's possible," I said, smiling. Leo looked at me with interest. I wondered what, if anything, Simeon had told him about me.

"Well, we have our imperfections. I'm not truly content with my job, and I've been too lazy to actually do anything about it. This is the year, though."

"You're doing better than me," I said. "At least you have a job." It occurred to me that I didn't know exactly what Simeon's job was.

He turned to Leo. "Now Leo, here, has a decent job. He's a bus driver. But his tragic flaw is that he rides a Harley. I mean…" Simeon looked disgusted, and Leo, who so far had said nothing, smiled ruefully.

Simeon focused his gaze on me. "Did you know that of all the Harleys ever made, ninety percent are still on the road?"

He looked at me with a twinkle as I shook my head.

"The rest made it home!" He barked with laughter.

I chuckled and moved on. Paul Butterfield was talking to someone I didn't know. I imagined Melanie was home with the kids, since babysitters were a rarity on New Year's Eve.

I made my way back to the bar for a refill. Desmond was breaking his usual on-duty abstinence and nursing a glass of Jamison's.

A burst of cold air indicated the door had opened, and several heads turned to see who the new arrival was.

It was Seth. He smiled at Desmond and slid out of his frayed coat. Desmond welcomed him and pointed to things that needed doing behind the bar. I couldn't hear their conversation, but their body language conveyed friendship, even affection.

Marta, freed from her labors, approached me with a

glass of some sort of cola.

"Is that Desmond's assistant?" I asked.

"Yes," she said. "A young guy who Desmond said really needed a job. His name is Seth something. Desmond says he's going to live upstairs. There's a tiny apartment up there that Desmond used when he first bought the place. Now he lives over in Newton."

Marta seemed particularly plugged in to Desmond's doings. I wondered briefly about that, saving for another day my own thoughts about having Seth living and working just down the road from me.

Marta excused herself and went to say something to Seth. I edged toward the back of the room. Roberta and Jim Bollinger had ended their discussion, and Jim was now talking with Paul.

Simeon and Leo had replenished their drinks and were chatting with Roberta, who looked more cheerful now that Jim Bollinger's attention was directed elsewhere. Simeon was, apparently, holding forth about his work day.

"So the relief valve is dripping. I tell the dude that if I can cut his water off for fifteen minutes, I can save him a plumbing bill, and myself a trip back.

"Moral: Buy a three-quarter-inch Wilkins, not the one-half."

Leo nodded sagely. So did Roberta, which surprised me somehow. Of course, just because I had no earthly idea about Simeon's profession, that didn't mean Roberta was just as ignorant.

A young man blocked my path. He had neatly groomed blond hair and wore a red and green plaid bow tie.

"Mademoiselle, my name is Roger. I would like to

wish you a Happy New Year."

He spoke very precisely, like one who is tilting into inebriation.

"And a Happy New Year to you. Now, if you'll excuse me…" I tried to go around him. But Roger matched my steps with sidesteps of his own, blocking my path. He was more agile than I would have thought.

Suddenly Seth stood between me and Roger. He steered me toward the bar. "Hope you don't mind. That guy is in here a lot, and frankly, he's a jerk."

I actually was pretty good at taking care of myself, but I didn't elaborate on that. I just thanked Seth for his consideration, and he returned to his duties.

Midnight was approaching, so I prepared my departure. I thanked Desmond for providing the venue, which of course was just good business on his part, but it felt like true hospitality. He looked surprised that I was leaving so soon but said nothing.

As I got into my coat, Roberta joined me and said she was heading home, too. We waved to the others. Several people shouted "Happy New Year!" as we went out into the cold.

She stopped just outside the door, before heading next door to her house.

"That Jim Bollinger," she said, shaking her head. "He is still angry at Graham, and the poor man is dead."

"Graham Farnsworth? What's Jim's beef with him?"

"Oh, Graham was a member of that historical foundation board I mentioned to you. He was not particularly diplomatic when he shot down Jim's proposal, almost sneering at the idea that Eliphalet Fenton even existed, much less had a historical role worthy of attention."

She sighed. "It's amazing how passionate people can be about these things, isn't it?"

We said our goodbyes and went our separate ways.

I was surprised, somehow, by how dark it was. There was no moon, and the stars glowed brightly once I had left the Star and Garter's illuminated parking lot.

I walked along the highway to the driveway and turned toward my house. The sound of my feet on the gravel was louder, or maybe more complex, somehow, than one person's footsteps. I stopped short and listened.

The footsteps continued for a few seconds, then stopped.

I considered whirling around and confronting whoever it was. Better to find out, or go into my house and be trapped? What if it was Roger?

I wished I'd brought a flashlight. I turned around and said, "Anybody there?"

A dark shape separated itself from the shadow along the driveway.

It was Simeon.

"Oh, it's you," I said, relieved and a bit annoyed at the same time. "I didn't realize you were coming home so early. Where's Leo?

"He's still back at the pub. I'm sorry I startled you. I just wanted to see you home safely."

Simeon and his mother hen behavior again.

If that's what it was.

"That's really nice of you, but really, you shouldn't bother."

I turned and went through the hedge opening and into my small yard. I unlocked my door and went in. I closed the door behind me and, before locking it, quietly opened it again, just a crack. I heard the gravel footsteps receding down the driveway. Simeon had, apparently fulfilled his chivalrous duty and was returning to the party.

I made myself comfortable on the loveseat and fired up the laptop. I found Times Square just as the spangled ball began to drop.

Chapter Twenty-Five

My house was shaping up, I had to admit. Even the lingering aroma of paint pleased me, suggesting as it did freshness and tender loving care. I'd climbed back onto my step ladder, trying to wrangle the curtain rod into the brackets I'd screwed into the molding. I hoped that if my natural tendency to stumble pitched me off the ladder, my natural tendency to get hooked on things might somehow be my salvation.

I had just settled the rod into the bracket when my phone rang. It was on the desk, so I climbed down as fast as I safely could and picked up.

"Miren? Mark here."

"Hi, how goes it?"

He seemed somewhat abrupt, dispensing with small talk. "Good, thanks. Listen, I want to ask you another small favor. I'm going to be over at that barn on the Pelham property near the veterans' cemetery. Remember that? The one they're fighting about renovating?"

"I think so," I said hesitantly. There was always a neglected historical building being fought over. It was hard to keep them straight. I thought I remembered that Farnsworth might have had an interest in the fate of the structure. I had the impression that he considered himself the savior of Bucks County's dwindling supply of classic barns.

"Well, this guy called and said he had a tip for me—he wouldn't elaborate, but said he needed to meet me at the property. It's probably related to the story I'm working on, so I can't afford to blow him off. All I need from you is a call in about half an hour…" He paused. "No, make that forty-five minutes. Say, two thirty. I should know then if there's something fishy."

"I can do that, but do you think this is a good idea? Couldn't he meet you in a more public place?"

"I know, I could have argued with him. But I have to check this out. I have no reason to feel there's anything wrong, but I'm just covering all bets here. All you need to do is call F.X. if I don't pick up."

"Sure we don't need a mysterious code word? If you whisper "sprezzatura" I know to call the police."

Mark chuckled and we signed off.

By the time I got the curtains up and hanging evenly, it was two thirty. I dialed Mark's cell.

No answer. It went to the mailbox.

Five minutes later, same thing.

I called F.X., but I reached his mailbox, too. I left a message and grabbed my car keys.

I pulled into the gravel driveway that led to the Pelham barn, wondering who or what had kept Mark from picking up, and whether that someone was still around. I didn't have time to park at a safe distance and make a stealthy approach to the barn, so I parked next to his gray Taurus. I got out and made a quick circle around the building.

It was a bank barn, like the one I'd seen from the towpath on my walk, but this one was a shambles. Broken windows, missing slates, saplings growing out of the gutters. The lower level walls were solid stone, and white paint peeled off the boards on the upper level.

I heard a rifle shot and jumped. Two more echoing shots followed. Then I remembered the veterans' cemetery. A burial must be taking place about half a mile to the south.

A door between the outer stalls and the barnyard stood open, so I went in. It was so much darker inside I could barely see the stalls in front of me.

A moan came from somewhere above. I called Mark's name. No answer.

Wooden steps led me up to the hayloft. At the top, I saw the hay shift slightly. I ran over and pulled it away.

Mark, pale and apparently dazed, was holding his right hand to his left shoulder. I knelt beside him.

"Shot," he said. His voice was hoarse. His eyes focused intently on mine.

Shot? I fumbled for my phone and thought about those rifle volleys.

I dialed 911, then looked more closely at Mark's shoulder. I saw nothing that looked like a gunshot wound.

We waited in the silence. Mark's eyes closed, and his breathing sounded shallow. I watched the dusty rays of light slant through the spaces between the boards in the barn wall.

Finally, the ambulance pulled up, and I ran downstairs to meet it.

"Just before he passed out, he said he was shot," I said, leading the EMTs to the loft. "But I didn't see any blood."

I stayed out of the way as they did their work. They

examined Mark, then lifted him gently and placed him on a collapsible gurney, buckling straps around him so they could angle him down the stairs. I didn't like the way he looked.

I followed the ambulance to the hospital and waited there until Mark's wife Elizabeth arrived. I called F.X. from the hospital, and this time he picked up. I explained what had happened.

Did he know what Mark was doing at the barn? Was it for a story? F.X. was just as perplexed as I was. There was nothing on the budget listing a Pelham story for tomorrow's paper, but Mark could have been working on something long-term. He tended to follow his own nose and did not always keep F.X. or Matt Papiernik informed.

When I got home from the hospital, I went upstairs to the closet and dug out the box of Elias' old camping gear where I'd stashed the thumb drive Mark had given me. I came back down and plugged it into the laptop.

There was one file on the drive. It was a video, labeled, "Sierra Vaca." *Vaca* is Spanish for cow, so I was a bit confused at first. Then I realized he'd abbreviated "vacation." I was pretty sure Mark hadn't given me a Nevada travelog. There was something on that drive that he wanted deniability about giving me.

I wasn't interested in travelogs, but I didn't know how Mark had arranged the video so I let it play. I adjusted the volume and picked up the sound of wind and traffic. It was indeed footage of the Sierra and the high plains, some taken from a car window. There were landscapes, dams, woods, and campsites, but no people.

The camera took me down a gravel road with houses and rural delivery mailboxes along one side.

Several names were visible, painted roughly in white on black metal boxes. Halverson. Pride. Bittner.

Suddenly the video broke up, and we were in a darkened room that appeared to be a restaurant. This looked like cell phone footage, taken on the sly.

One man in the picture looked vaguely familiar, but the other, facing him across the table and with his back to the camera, was nothing more than a grainy silhouette.

The visible man said, "The key to this is keeping the place full."

The second man laughed. "That's your department."

A woman approached the table with a tray, only her mid-section visible. She put two glasses on the table. They looked like mixed drinks in highball glasses. The second man said, "Thanks, sweetheart." Their faces turned toward her as she walked away.

Second man: Look, there's a lot to be done. Place is a wreck. We got trees growing out of the main section. I can't pour money into this unless it's a sure thing.

First man: How nice does it have to be? Lots of these kids get sent out to wilderness camps.

Second man: Oh, it'll be no-frills boarding school style. I've done this before. Approvals are cake. If I know what's coming, I can have this up and running within a couple months. Meantime, I got room for them upstate.

They were, apparently, talking about the Wintergreen property and a highly undesirable—if not illegal—use planned for it. The conversation turned to numbers that I guessed were dollar amounts. The first man, who I suspected was an official of some sort, appeared to dial his cell phone. Then he announced a number, and I realized he was using the calculator function. They lifted their drinks and clinked their glasses.

The video ended.

****

Elizabeth Calabrese, Mark's wife, called me that afternoon. "They don't know anything more, except they think he may have been drugged. You mentioned that he said he was shot, and that he was clutching his right shoulder? They checked and found a needle mark. They're doing a whole battery of tests right now."

"A needle mark? As in a hypodermic? They were saying someone gave him a shot?"

"Apparently."

"Jeesh. How does he seem, Elizabeth?"

"Completely comatose. No sign of anything. They have him on IV fluids, but he's breathing and all his vital signs are strong." She paused. "I don't know what to think.

"All I can do is thank you for finding him, Miren. I don't know what would have happened if you hadn't rushed over there."

Someone was determined to keep Mark from finishing that article. I thought about the men in the restaurant. I put the thumb drive back in the camping box and checked that my doors were locked

Chapter Twenty-Six

Stephen Melchior was on the phone. "Any chance you could come by the department? I could show you what we were working on. And you could bring those specimens along. Mia is here all afternoon, if you could come by today."

"I guess I can," I said. "I'd be happy to move ahead on clearing out specimens. I just got rid of Elias's instruments, so I'm on a roll."

There was a pause. "You sold them to Lawrence?"

"Yes."

"I told you not to do that!"

His voice was harsh. Evidently Stephen had a temper, and an irrational one at that.

My surprise quickly turned to impatience. "Excuse me. I mentioned that possibility, and you said you had no problem with it. You saw everything I had."

He was silent, so I filled the gap with my usual blurt. "If you have some information about why I should do something or not do something, would you be kind enough to share it with me, instead of dicking around with all these hints and guessing games, and then criticizing me when I guess wrong?"

His silence continued. And then he said, "You're right. I'm conflicted about this whole thing, and my dealings with you are reflecting that."

"Conflicted how?" I asked.

"Can you get over here today? We can talk, and Mia can have some input, too. I think it's time I tell you why I have certain suspicions. Not of you, I can assure you."

He gave me directions to the lab and signed off. I began packing the sheets of mounting paper with ancient, moldy pine needles glued to them. It would be nice to get them cleared out, especially if they were of use to anyone.

I found Stephen's building easily enough but had to circle for quite a while before finding a place to park. I finally succeeded and carried my unwieldy carton back to his building.

He had a small office next to the laboratory he shared with Mia Sung. He brought me coffee, which he remembered I took black. It wasn't very good.

He cleared a stack of journals and reprints off a chair and invited me to sit. He sat behind his desk.

He took a breath and began. "Lawrence Shaw's father was a chemist here. He died last spring, but for about a year before that, he was working with your uncle on a possible pharmaceutical application of the fungal metabolites. They'd been putting together a grant proposal to fund further studies. There was a possibility of generous support, which was pretty tempting.

"As I told you, Eugene had noted some similarities between certain fungus intermediates and antibiotics. He thought it might possibly lead to a new class of drugs, something that's desperately needed.

"But when he studied the material in its impure state, it acted entirely differently—more like a hard-hitting general anesthetic.

"And then Eugene died. That left Elias with a big gap in the endeavor. We all hoped he could continue the project on his own, with a little help from the rest of us.

"And then your uncle died suddenly. It was about that time that Lawrence started showing up here more frequently than one would expect. We all felt sorry for him after his father died. His mother died long ago, I think.

"But he seemed to be acting oddly. He showed a lot of interest in your uncle's work, which was understandable since Elias and his father had been collaborating. But he kept coming in and just hanging around, to the point that it seemed creepy.

"I don't know why he's interested in your uncle's equipment, Miren. It may be perfectly true that he wants it for his classroom. But I don't trust him, because it's possible he's after something else."

He drained his coffee cup. I lifted mine to my lips, but it was nearly cold.

Finally, I asked Stephen about Elias' position at the university. He leaned back in his chair and seemed glad to be done with the subject of Lawrence.

"Elias was an adjunct," he said, "which means he was essentially a temp, and not paid much. But he had privileges, as it were. He had unlimited access to the building and the lab.

"He had a wealth of experience and knowledge in the field and was respected by mycologists all over the world. It was assumed he'd use our equipment for some of his work and then share his findings with us. He published several papers with me and Eugene. It's not a bad arrangement, really—using private experts who are eager to pursue their work for their own personal satisfaction.

"Your uncle was the only one who knew the location of the fungus source in the wild. My sense was that without Elias' maps and knowledge of the habitat, the proposal couldn't be completed. And any commercial application would depend on an adequate supply, at least until the compound could be synthesized."

Ah. Was that why Lawrence offered to buy the map file? I wondered if Lawrence wanted more from my house than just antique lab equipment. I thought about the Bartram letters. I thought about possible hiding places for fungus spores, places I hadn't thought of, and what I would do if I actually found them.

"Suppose I were to find this scary fungus somewhere on my property?" I asked. "How do scientists analyze something that might be toxic, but might not? How do they begin—and avoid poisoning themselves?"

"Well," he said, "if you know enough to know it might be hazardous, you take standard precautions. There are three basic routes of exposure—through the skin, through inhalation and through ingestion. So if you don't eat the stuff, and if you wear gloves and a proper respirator, you should be okay.

"The problem is when you don't have any reason to be suspicious of a sample. Then it's possible to get in serious trouble."

The door from the hallway to the laboratory opened, and a tall Asian woman who appeared to be in her thirties walked in. She was wearing a navy pea jacket and carrying a grocery bag from the Pennington

Market.

She called out a greeting to Stephen. He got up from his chair, and said to me, "Let's have Mia take a look at these." He grabbed my carton and led me through the laboratory into her office.

Stephen introduced us, and Mia made the usual expressions of condolence. I thanked her, and explained that all I had heard from my family was that Elias fell at work and never regained consciousness.

She nodded and indicated a chair in front of the desk. Stephen remained standing, leaning against the wall.

"Your uncle was working alone," Mia said, "and apparently had a fall in the old storeroom where we keep deaccessioned specimens, old ones that no longer belong in the active files. Most of them could be disposed of, but there are regulations for any kind of biological material. We can't just throw it in a dumpster, so it has to be kept until certain procedures are complete.

"Hardly anyone goes down there, but Elias enjoyed rummaging through them, like an archaeologist. The janitorial staff never thought to look there, and it wasn't until after weeks had passed that his body was found on the floor."

"As you may have gathered," I said, glancing at Stephen, "I didn't get much information from our family. All they said was that he had some kind of heart failure. Did you learn anything more about a cause of death?"

Mia shook her head. "There was no indication of an injury serious enough to keep him from seeking help had he been conscious.

"It was very sad," she said, shaking her head. "How awful to think of a kindly old man dying alone like that."

She turned to the carton of specimens and began to look through them as Stephen and I waited in silence. She studied them for a long time, turning from time to time to type data into her computer. As she worked she set a few aside.

Finally, she turned to me and said, "Most of these are duplicates of items we have in our collection, but some I'd like to keep. You can dispose of the rest if you wish; as a private citizen, you don't have to follow any particular procedures. I can assure you they're quite harmless unless you have a mold allergy."

I thanked Mia, and we said our goodbyes. Stephen and I took the elevator down to the ground floor. I was carrying the carton of pine needles; I figured it would make sense to dispose of them at home, as a private citizen, rather than complicate life for the department's janitors.

"Thank you for filling me in on my uncle's work, and all the complexities of the project," I said. "I'm not sure I understand where it's going if it's going anywhere at all. Is there a chance you yourself might step in?"

He gazed thoughtfully through the glass doors into the fading late afternoon light.

"Unlikely. I'm a geneticist, and the project would need a chemist and a biologist. Plus, without your uncle's material, and the precise location where he collected it, there may not be much point."

He held the door for me and stepped back inside. I headed out into the dusk.

I walked down Duke Street and was about to turn left toward my car when a familiar voice called out to me.

I turned. It was Lawrence. Lawrence seemed to turn up a lot these days.

He suggested coffee and gestured to a corner shop called the Aardvark. I was impressed that Lawrence had discovered another coffee shop that met his high standards.

Once again, I was wary, but accepted the offer. I realized I actually enjoyed the company of people who are hard to please. I had learned, from long experience with prickly people, how to tiptoe around them so as to keep the social interaction going without incurring their disapproval. I'd learned how to expertly fan the flames of discourse without extinguishing it altogether or fanning it into a runaway conflagration.

So I found that aspect of Lawrence somewhat pleasing. Being with a person of high standards felt right.

The Aardvark reflected an earlier era of coffee houses—dim, somewhat dusty, with a blackboard on an easel advertising the week's menu of musicians. Friday featured the bi-weekly poetry slam. One side of the room was clear of tables, and a stool and sound equipment stood against the wall.

We ordered our usual, and Lawrence said, "What's in the box?"

I lied, not very gracefully. "Oh, just some papers. It's a long story." I was going to ask him if he'd had a pleasant holiday but stopped myself. It occurred to me that Lawrence might have had a very lonely Christmas. As odd as he occasionally was, he deserved a certain amount of pity as an orphan. But he must have thought the same about me and came up with a neutral workaround.

"So," he said, "have you ever been to the Crossing?"

For a moment, I thought he meant Fenton's Crossing, but quickly realized he meant the Christmas Day reenactment.

"I did," I said. "It was cold, but very enjoyable. It was actually quite moving."

"Did George give his speech, that Thomas Paine thing from 'Common Cause'?"

I hesitated for just a fraction of a second before correcting him. "From 'The American Crisis,' yes he did. Very affecting."

" 'The American Crisis,' Lawrence responded, in a slightly impatient tone that suggested, "That's what I said."

Lawrence really didn't like being wrong. Most people are able to laugh off occasional slips and stumbles. Lawrence, apparently, had to shuffle the situation to make himself right.

He reminded me of some of the commenters on the blog. Two stubborn, knowledgeable people going at it hammer and tongs, information and citations exploding outward like sparks from an anvil. First one would be ascendant, then the other would reach for a statistic and flip his opponent like a wrestler on a mat.

Finally, when one of them seemed pinned, defeated, he would go fractal. He wouldn't admit error. He would change the scale, zeroing in on a tiny detail where He Was Right.

I realized this was what Lawrence was doing. He

really needed, absolutely had, to be Right.

He pronounced Nevada Right. He was Right about which coffee shop to patronize. He was Right about Thomas Paine.

As we finished our coffee and stood to go, Lawrence asked about the *Clarion* and how Spencer and Mark were doing on their stories. He seemed to think they were his pals, though they'd met just once at Krakatoa.

I answered in general terms, revealing only what had already been in the paper. I certainly said nothing about Mark's misfortune, and how it had delayed the publication of his story.

I ducked into the bathroom before leaving, so Lawrence waited at the table. When I came back, I saw him drop one of the flaps of the carton back into place. The little sneak.

As I slipped my shoulder bag on and hoisted my carton, Lawrence offered to carry the box back to my car. I thanked him, but said I had to make one stop before that, and we said good bye. It occurred to me that I was fibbing more than usual these days.

It was quite dark when I got home. I stopped the car at the end of the driveway to toss the carton into Marta's trash bin. I felt a certain trepidation as I pulled into my yard and opened my door.

For the first time, being alone felt cold, almost sinister.

Someone had killed Farnsworth. Mark had been attacked and injected with something mysterious that disabled him. My own great-uncle had died under unusual circumstances. Seth's behavior was peculiar, if not suspicious. And somebody was drifting in and out of my house like a ghost. I determined to watch my back until these loose ends were tied up.

Too many people seemed like possible villains: Lawrence and his avid interest in antique scientific equipment, plus his interest in fungus: Seth with his lock-picking tools: Stephen and his temper. I felt so off balance that I was beginning to suspect people who weren't, by any reasonable assessments, suspicious at all. Quite a few people had been in my house. Some of the suspects were husky enough to handle the gallows gambit. Ezra? Kevin? Simeon? Pradip? Desmond? Hell, what about Edmond Greenwood? And who knows, maybe Marta was stronger than she looked. Maybe the Butterfields' baby was really, really strong.

People seemed to be losing consciousness in places where they weren't likely to be found. Solitary places. In Elias' case, they died. In Mark's case, I hoped not, but it was hard to know.

That night, I lay in bed, thinking the thoughts of the solitary person. What if I lost consciousness, just blanked out? How long would it take before I was found and given medical attention?

Probably about twenty minutes, I thought wryly, given the frisky neighborliness of Fenton's Crossing. Somebody would break into my house, or just peek in my windows. Maybe Marta would check in, or Simeon would drop by to borrow a cup of sugar.

Was it such a good idea to see so much of Stephen and Lawrence? Our meetings were nothing more than business appointments, plus a lot of coffee. But if either of them escalated the relationship, I'd have to explain my policy about entanglements, never an easy conversation to have.

Usually, I resented it when men demonstrated an interest despite my standoffish behavior. At other times, I loosened the reins on my mind and allowed myself to imagine what it would be like to be someone's treasure.

Chapter Twenty-Seven

Next morning, I was awakened by my cell phone. It was Elizabeth. Her voice was shaking with excitement. "Mark's awake! He's weak but seems okay. He wants to talk to you."

"Oh, that's awesome! Does he remember what happened?"

"No," she said. "Either he's blanked it out, or whoever attacked him came from behind; he doesn't know who it was."

I said I'd be right over.

It was wonderful to see him sitting up. He was a little gaunt, and still in a hospital gown, but his crisp hair was combed and he'd been freshly shaved. Elizabeth was seated in a bedside chair, her hand in his.

"He can go home tomorrow," she said, beaming.

I asked Mark if he felt up to talking. He nodded. "First," he said, "I have to thank you for coming to my rescue."

I told him about finding him in the barn and said that after he'd been taken to the hospital, I went home and watched the video on the thumb drive he'd given me.

Rather than ask him to explain the whole story to me, I said, "Mark, you were assaulted. Maybe because of the story. You need to be really careful."

He nodded. "The best way to do that is to publish

the story. Whoever did this has to be one of those guys you saw in the video, or some goon of theirs."

I asked Elizabeth if there was some way the hospital could withhold information about Mark's release—or even delay it. Maybe he could finish the story from his hospital room.

Mark looked thoughtful. "I'll call F.X. and see what he and Abraham Wilberforce think. Maybe we can work something out with hospital security and I can finish the story here. I'm that close."

****

The moon was nearly full. The night was quiet and soft, even though it was February. I pulled a chair next to my upstairs east window and sat with a glass of a nice rosé from Languedoc and thought about fungus. About Seth. About Mark's story. About maps and letters. About toothbrushes and keys.

The road on the Jersey bank sparkled with occasional car headlights. I glanced at the surface of the river, which had been low for weeks. It looked a bit higher. I watched as a small branch moved on the surface. A piece of what looked like plywood slid along next to it. It seemed to have some kind of rough lettering on it, but it was hard to see in the gloom.

And I sat up. And stared. I watched the branch and plywood for a moment, moving my head from right to left.

The river was flowing backward.

Chapter Twenty-Eight

I rubbed my eyes and watched for a while. Once my initial surprise passed, my rational self told me there had to be a reason. Either it was an illusion, or the tide reversed the river's flow under certain circumstances. There had to be an explanation. I would pursue it in the morning. I closed up the house and went to bed.

As I lay staring at the ceiling, I thought about things going in reverse, turning counterclockwise. Time running the wrong way, effect and cause all out of synch.

I knew that my pattern, my salvation, really, was to look ahead, to forge ahead in one direction. I knew that I couldn't undo the past, no matter how much I dwelled on it. It was how I had survived the trauma of my child's birth and death, my mother's abandonment, trying to survive on my own and, even on a certain level, managing to be successful.

But somehow that wasn't serving me well. There's a lot about psychology I don't buy, especially its emphasis on facing and understanding one's traumas. But now I wondered if my strategy of freezing the past, damming it behind huge blocks of ice, was really working for me.

My mind wandered to the snares and tangles that bound my spirit, along with the real tangles that made me trip. Those honeysuckle vines had ensnared me when I got out of my car along the river. I remembered unlacing myself from them, patiently pulling my feet backward. Sometimes the only way to untangle yourself is to stop pressing forward, and back up.

During the long years it took me to get through college, I once interned on the copy desk of the Reno paper that later hired me. One of my colleagues showed me a trick when you're reading closely. You work backward, word by word and line by line. That way you aren't lulled by the meaning of the text, which can cause you to overlook errors.

Maybe backing up had something going for it. Maybe the time had come to stop pushing forward. Maybe it was time to go back to the beginning.

I got out of bed, slipped on my woolen robe and rummaged among the tent stakes in the closet for the thumb drive. Then I went down the stairs and opened Mark's file again.

I sped through the Nevada part of the video until it got to the narrow road with the mailboxes. Something about that scene had stuck in my mind, but I couldn't remember what because I was anticipating Mark's footage, hurrying through to reach the important stuff. I could almost smell the scent of pine and juniper as the boughs nearly brushed against the windshield.

The mailboxes appeared, with white letters on dark metal. Smith. Garcia. Halverson. Pride.

That was it. Pride. I paused the video. Barbara Pride was the sister wife who attended me at the birth of my child. She was Elder Morrow's wife, of course, but she had told me her maiden name. It was unlikely this mailbox belonged to her; it was most likely a coincidence. But it made me think I needed to try to track her down and see if she would talk to me.

I made a pot of coffee and got back to work.

With the help of Google and some reporter research tricks, I located her in Winnemucca. I wished I had an email address for my initial approach to her, because most people are less spooked by an email from a long-lost stranger than a cold phone call.

Finally, I concluded I'd have to go with the telephone and hope to leave a message. I'd wait until around one p.m., which would be about ten a.m. Nevada Time—the time most working people are out, and I'd be more likely to reach her voice mail.

I dug up news reports about what happened after the compound was raided and closed. I located Benjamin Morrow in Ely State Prison, as Seth had indicated. I wondered who else had gone to jail. Would there be child endangerment charges against the women, or would they be viewed as victims? I wasn't able to find many answers.

I stood and stretched. I was ready to call it a night, but remembered I had to find out what was wrong with my river.

A quick search of "tidal rivers" told me that in certain unusual circumstances, when low water levels in the river occur at the same time as a particularly high tide at sea, a tidal river can flow backward much farther upstream than usual. This backwash, or bore, usually happened father downstream, off Philadelphia. It was unusual for it to come this far upriver, but that's what it had done.

No magic. No hallucinations. Just the way the real world, my world, worked.

Dawn was breaking over New Jersey and finding

its way to my window. I went upstairs and collapsed on the bed.

Chapter Twenty-Nine

My message to Barbara Pride was brief, but I hoped not alarming. I gave her my name and number and said I had been in touch with Seth Morrow. Would she be willing to contact me?

She called back that afternoon. She expressed amazement at hearing from me but seemed reluctant to say much right away.

"How is Seth?" she asked. Her voice, always gentle, had aged over the years.

"Actually, I don't know him that well. I was hoping you could provide some background."

There was silence. "Could we include him on the call?"

"I'll ask him. If I can find him."

She said I could call her as soon as I found him. We agreed to use Skype for the conversation. We hung up,

Seth's presence during the conversation didn't bother me, but I still didn't want him in my house.

I walked into the Star and Garter and bellied up to the bar. Desmond's face brightened when he turned away from the beer pumps and saw me. He knew my preference by now and slid a small Harp toward me. I asked how business was going.

"I've a steady stream of custom, but one doesn't grow wildly successful from beer alone," he said. "I dream of adding a lunch menu; you know, pub food. But the permits! The delays! They're a terrible burden, so they are."

When I'd drunk half my Harp, I posed my question. "I was wondering if you could get a message to Seth Morrow."

"I could indeed. What shall it be?"

"I need to talk to him. Could you ask him to meet me here?"

His eyes flickered with curiosity. After all, Desmond had no clue about my connection with Seth. Or at least I thought he didn't.

But he just glanced at his watch. "He's agreed to help me with the barrels later today, maybe about four. You could come back then, if it suits you."

I agreed to do that. Then I asked Desmond if we might borrow his back room for a Skype conversation later on. He agreed, and I put some bills on the bar and left.

****

At four, I returned in the car, with my laptop on the passenger seat. I'd texted Barbara Pride, suggesting sometime between one and one thirty her time. She responded and said she'd be waiting.

I sat at the bar and waited. Soon Seth came up the narrow stairs from the basement, where the kegs were set up. He seemed pleased to see me, if a bit wary.

"I've tracked Sister Barbara down. Do you remember her?"

His eyes widened. "Do I remember her? She raised me."

"I'm sorry. Of course. Well, she's in Nevada and willing to talk about what happened at the compound.

She suggested Skype. And she asked how you were, and if you could be on the call." I wondered if he'd chicken out. After all, the likelihood was that whatever he learned would be a devastating disappointment.

But he looked pleased, if a bit surprised. "Um, yeah. I guess. When do you want to do this?"

"Right now, if that's okay with you."

I felt a pang of guilt about springing this on Seth with no warning. I'd had a day or so to think about the upcoming conversation with Barbara Pride, and he'd had no time at all.

We set up in the back room that Desmond used as a little office. It held cases of beer and cleaning supplies, along with his desk. I set the laptop on a small table and plugged in the power cord.

We called the number Barbara had given me and waited.

A series of blinking rectangles appeared on the screen, and the picture formed itself. I saw a familiar face, much aged, but with the same dark eyes and sharp nose I remembered. Her once-dark hair was mostly gray now, and her face was worn. Behind her on the wall, I could see knotty pine paneling and a round wall clock that showed 1:18.

I wasn't all that used to Skype, and it took a while to sink in that she could see us just as well, with a stack of empty beer kegs behind us. Then her face changed, transforming from solemn to radiant.

"Seth," she breathed. Her hand reached out toward us. Her eyes were shiny. "Seth. You're all grown up."

"And Miren." She dabbed at her eye with a tissue.

"Hello, Barbara," I said. Seth just nodded.

"I'm sorry," she said. "It's just getting to me.

Seeing the two of you together."

"Take your time," I said. "We're just grateful that you're willing to talk to us about all this."

"Seth, I was so sorry when everything came to an end. I've wondered about you ever since. Miren, I...if only you hadn't run away. I've been having trouble coming to terms with that period of my life, and I've finally been able to make some changes."

I wondered about Barbara's life after the compound, and what changes she'd made. But now was not the time to ask.

"But no matter how out of our minds we were while we were living there as sister wives, you should know we really were devastated when the baby was born dead. And of course, Elder Morrow was so counting on a son born to you," she said.

Would Seth believe me now? His face was expressionless.

Barbara cleared her throat and began her story. She told how Elder Morrow believed I was a kind of prophesied wife or handmaiden, destined to deliver the son who would carry forth his mission. I'd never been clear on what that mission was, but I knew it was partly religious and partly militantly anti-government.

She told us about my pregnancy, and how anticipated it was. How my mother had disappeared. She described my labor and the birth. It was hard to listen to, but it matched my own memories.

"After we'd taken the baby from you, we moved him to the supply trailer. We were shaken up; we didn't know what to tell Elder Morrow. When I came back, you were having another contraction; the placenta was being expelled. You needed to push a bit, but you weren't cooperating. You'd given up, I think. Finally, it emerged, with some help from us.

"And there, tangled in the bloody tissue, was a tiny, tiny baby. A twin."

I sensed a gate slam shut deep within, a vain effort to keep something out. But it was no use.

"I was so sure this second baby was dead that I scooped it up, along with the placenta, and rushed it to the trailer. I didn't think you could stand to see another dead baby."

"Sister Anne stayed with you and got you cleaned up. You were in and out of consciousness. You'd had an awful time.

"I remember I was crying as I wrapped him for burial, and at first I didn't trust what I saw. But I saw his chest move. He seemed to be trying to breathe. I looked around for something to suction him with but ended up using my mouth. Then I breathed carefully into his mouth. He gave a tiny, weak cry, more of a gasp, really. I didn't know what to do—he was unlikely to live or be healthy even if he did. I wrapped him as warmly as I could. I said a prayer for him.

"When I went back, you were sleeping, or had passed out. I told Sister Ann what had happened. We decided to keep it from you for the time being, and even from Elder Morrow. We didn't think he would live. Of course, looking back, I realize we should have taken him to a hospital, even though it would take an hour to get there.

"You were pretty weak for the first day or so, Miren. You'd lost a lot of blood, and you seemed to be beyond caring about anything.

"Then the third—I think third—morning, we went

into the infirmary to check on you. You were gone.

"By that time, the baby looked stronger. I'd kept him warmly wrapped, and he took a little formula. Every time I went back, I expected him to be dead, but he was always alive, moving, getting pinker every day.

"We went to Elder Morrow and told him what had happened. He was ecstatic, and furious at the same time because we'd kept it from him. He insisted we get medical help. He determined that we would raise the baby, and that we were all better off with you out of our lives. You had given him what he wanted.

"So we made it official. We listed the mother's name as Mary Morrow on the birth certificate. We never mentioned the first baby to anyone.

"And, I've been saying 'him' when I talk about that baby. But of course, that was you, Seth. Somehow you made it. You grew up. And here you are."

She stopped.

"Miren, you look stunned. Do you want to contact me later when you've absorbed all this?"

I looked at Seth. My mind was racing. If what Barbara said was true, and her memory accurate, I was looking at a son I never knew I had. He met my glance for a second, then turned back to the screen.

They spoke briefly—Barbara eagerly asking Seth about his life, willing him to have had a good one; Seth solemnly trying to answer. At least I think so; I wasn't paying close attention. There was a buzzing in my mind…

We agreed to talk again later. I exited the program and heard myself sigh, a long breath. I looked at Seth. He looked at me. It was beginning to look as if he was right, and he was my son. This was not something I was prepared to deal with just yet, but I had to accept the likelihood that my whole adult life had been an illusion. I was accepting it in my mind, but my heart wasn't convinced.

Seth spoke. He had a way of measuring his words, rarely blurting them out.

"You know," he said quietly, "they have DNA testing. I'm not saying we have to do it, but you shouldn't make up your mind about anything until it's determined."

It was absurd, really. You hear all the time about men who find out later in life that they had a child from a casual relationship. But a woman? How can a woman have a child she doesn't know exists?

I was running out of thoughts, feelings, energy. "So what do we do now?" I asked.

"Nothing," he said. "I keep working for Desmond; I stick around but I don't get in your way?"

He was clearly being solicitous of my feelings, which made sense since I had had the greater shock. But what about his feelings? He had just, apparently, found his long-lost mother. And what an unwelcoming, poor excuse for a mother he'd found!

And yet his first thought was for me and my feelings. Something in me had to like him for that.

He slid back his chair and got up from the table. He took two steps away and snagged the toe of his sneaker in a loop of the power cord. He stumbled but caught himself.

I knew.

****

From the archives of *The Elk City Echo*
September 6, 2006

A man charged with polygamy and a number of firearms violations has been sentenced to 17 years in state prison on two of the charges. He awaits sentencing on two federal convictions.

Benjamin Morrow, 52, the leader of a cult in rural Pershing County, was convicted in July of charges stemming from his activities at the cult's compound. According to trial testimony, he married several wives and, in some cases, prevented members from leaving the compound. He also had amassed a large arsenal of weapons, in preparation to doing battle with government forces, according to trial testimony.

Chapter Thirty

My first morning as a mother dawned bitter and cold. I could feel the frigid air through my windows; the panes on the western side, where the sun hadn't yet struck, were decorated with ornate frost patterns, veined and scalloped like geranium leaves.

Seth and I had parted yesterday as tentative strangers. Neither of us felt related to the other, just yet. He went back to work hauling Desmond's kegs up from the basement, and I went home to think.

Over the past twenty years, I had found myself noticing children, boys in particular. The only ones who caught my attention were the age my son would have been had he lived. At first I noticed only babies, then, as the years passed, toddlers, then school-age children, then teenagers. I'd be thinking I'd put that part of my life out of my mind, but then a boy would appear and, unbidden, I would find myself speculating: What would my child have been like?

So when I saw the thin kid with the silver backpack walking along the railroad track behind the *Clarion*, I wanted to grab him. Get off that track, I thought. Danger.

And now that thin kid turned out to be my real-life son. I felt no particular attachment to him, beyond that lingering protective impulse. I had no responsibility to him. No obligation, economically or, I assumed, legally. He was an adult. But emotionally? I had to be available in some way, be the mother he'd finally found. Such as she was.

I had no idea what I wanted. If anything. As to what Seth wanted, well, the logical thing to do was ask him. But not yet.

After coffee and a bowl of oatmeal, my Western pragmatism kicked in. I was ready to investigate the medical aspects of Barbara's story, which seemed plausible and yet somehow mystifying. I'd heard about oddities in twin gestation and remembered hearing that many single pregnancies start out with twins, but one embryo is reabsorbed. I'd never paid much attention to these issues. I needed to know what had happened to me—and Seth—two decades ago.

Rather than aimlessly search medical sites, I went to my familiar blog.

Occam's Laser and Mrs. Calabash were there, arguing about the merits of 1970s bands I'd never heard of. Zelda was worried that her basement would flood in the storm that was headed her way, which I thought— but couldn't be sure—was somewhere in North Carolina.

Basquette Case: Morning, all. Good luck, Zelda.

Zelda: Thanks, B.C. Trouble is, we often lose power in these parts. If it floods, my sump pump goes dark.

Grendel: You can just start a fish farm down there.

Mrs. Calabash: Carpe diem!

Occam's Laser: Don't forget to check the gefilte in the sump pump.

Several LOLs and digital eyerolls ensued.

Basquette Case: I have a medical question for the

hive mind.

Grendel: Dr. Death Panel was here earlier. Shall we summon him?

Dr. Death Panel: Yo.

Basquette Case: Does anyone know the term for the prenatal condition in which twins are very different in size? One unusually large, the other very small. Can be life-threatening.

Doctor Death Panel: B.C., that's called twin transfusion syndrome. It's rare, fortunately, and affects only monozygotic (identical) twins that share a placenta. Gimme a minute and I'll dig up a web site for you.

A few minutes later, he came back with a link. I thanked him and left the blog.

I took a breath and put myself in reporter mode. I went to the site, and learned that in some twin pregnancies, the shared placenta enables a connection between the blood supply of the two fetuses, and one becomes a blood donor for the other. The larger twin is at risk for hypertension, and the donor for anemia. If the condition is discovered in time, treatment is effective; it usually involves the use of lasers to sever the link between the blood vessels of the fetuses.

The impossible became just a bit more possible.

****

Mark's story hit the lawns and driveways of thousands of subscribers Sunday morning. It was posted on the website at midnight.

He'd texted ahead of time to let me know, and I was all set to read it first thing.

I made coffee and let it steep while I fired up the laptop.

It was a three-part series. Part one was headlined:

County Judge, Juvenile Prison Developer
Target of FBI Probe

by Mark Calabrese
Clarion Staff Writer

County and Federal prosecutors are investigating allegations that County Judge Winston Farragut accepted nearly $1 million to railroad hundreds of juvenile defendants and send them to a private detention facility, sources tell the Clarion.

According to the sources, authorities are also investigating James Bennington, whose company maintains private prisons specializing in juvenile inmates.

County assistant District Attorney Claire Sorber said she could not confirm or deny any investigation "at this point in time."

A staff member at Judge Farragut's office, who asked not to be identified, said the judge was taking personal leave and would not be available for comment.

The Clarion's six-month investigation began when the mother of a Bucks County youth incarcerated in Bennington's facility in rural Pennsylvania approached the paper with her concerns about what she called the lack of due process in juvenile court cases.

"My son was no angel, but they didn't have to send him away," said Maureen Conway of Billington. "They got him for trespassing. Skateboarding on someone's parking lot. We showed up in court and the judge wouldn't let his lawyer even speak before convicting him and sentencing him to prison.

"For skateboarding."

The juveniles were sent to Bennington's existing facility in the north-central part of the state. Bennington is currently rehabilitating the Wintergreen tract in Hampton Township to house additional inmates.

A courthouse employee, who also requested anonymity, said Farragut, who as president judge controls the court's budget, abruptly cut off funding for the county facility that has housed juveniles for decades. He then used the deteriorating condition of that facility to promote the need for privately run prisons.

Sources close to the investigation say Bennington and Farragut put the financial aspects of their deal in writing; the large sums of money transferred triggered federal charges.

Jonathan Fenster, chief of the public defender's office, said his staff has complained for the past year that judge Farragut has dismissed their pleas for leniency, and in some cases barred them from speaking or acting on their clients' behalf. In many of these cases, Fenster said, the juvenile posed no threat and could have remained in his home community.

He said before the county detention facility was closed a few months ago, he was told that the court would tell staff how many inmates to expect at the end of each day—even before the trials were conducted.

Farragut had a reputation as a particularly strict judge, one who advocated a philosophy of "Tough Love."

I had to stop reading for a while. I stood and paced. A kid had been hauled before juvenile court, represented by a harried, confused public defender who couldn't figure out why all his clients got sent up the river. A kid who had done nothing worse than Seth had, and possibly a lot less. Kids who probably needed a stern lecture and a few weekends of community service but were sent away from their homes and families and into the tender mercies of a monster.

The story described the arrangement between Farragut and Bennington, who had not only committed their deal to paper, they had conducted meetings in public places like the restaurant where Mark recorded their public conversation.

I called Mark on his cell to congratulate him on the story and see how he was doing. Did he feel safe? Was the District Attorney going to look into the assault he'd suffered and question Farragut and Bennington? Was there any news from the toxicology people about the nature of his injection?

Mark said he felt safe enough, safe enough to leave the hospital, now that the story was out. There was a huge spotlight shining on the bad guys, and he suspected they would stay out of trouble until their arrests, which Mark suspected would be soon.

"Oh…" he continued "…about the toxicology report. They're kind of baffled. All they could find was a lot of histamine and antibodies to a toxin that's only found in certain molds and fungi."

****

If someone was injecting newspaper reporters with toxic fungus, there had to be a reason. And if the fungus in question was Elias', someone had to have access to the material, along with a motive. Lawrence? Stephen? Mia? The judge in Mark's investigative piece?

I wanted to talk to Mia Sung again. I remembered

Elias' old photos taken at the laboratory, at parties and professional gatherings, and I figured she'd know who'd want them. That gave me an excuse to drop by the department.

Mia welcomed me warmly and was delighted to see the photos. I asked her about the grant proposal. "Would it be worth trying to put together your own team to continue the work?"

"Well, Elias' work was unique. Nobody else focused on those organisms. Also, we have a teaching load, and Elias didn't.

"And, of course, he didn't have a family, which made things easier—" She caught herself and rephrased: "I'm sorry. Of course he had family. I meant that he lived alone."

"No problem," I said. "I know what you mean. How about you and Stephen, if that's not too personal? Do you have families?"

She smiled and reached behind her for a framed photo on the shelf. She handed it to me, and I studied the face of a very cute toddler with sparkling brown eyes.

"That's Sophie," Mia said. "My husband is a lawyer, and his schedule is as bad as mine. When we have time, we go kayaking or back country hiking. There's never enough time, though.

"Now, Stephen is divorced, but he has shared custody of his son. So he's a little less overbooked than me."

I asked her if she knew anything about how the fungus was supposed to work as an anesthetic. She said that, unfortunately, Shaw was the expert on that, along with a research pharmacist he'd consulted with. She couldn't remember his name, but said she'd let me know if she did.

I understood that everyone was busy, but it seemed odd that nobody showed much interest in pursuing the project. It seemed a shame to just jettison something that might have great value. But then, I wasn't familiar with how the scientific mind—or the scientific bureaucracy—worked.

On the way home, my phone chirped. It was a text from Spencer, asking me to call him. As a law-abiding citizen, I waited until I'd gotten home and parked the car to make the call.

"Miren, just a heads up, but you're attracting attention."

"In what way?"

"I'm not sure, but it doesn't seem to be about the Farnsworth investigation. It's the attack on Mark. Apparently they got a tip from someone. Said you had access to the toxin used against Mark."

Words failed me for a moment. Then I told Spencer about my uncle's research. "But even if his was the same toxin used to attack Mark, it couldn't have been me. I have no idea where he hid his sample."

Spencer was silent.

"Plus, what possible motivation would I have? I went out to that barn to help Mark, not hurt him."

"I have no idea, Miren. I'll keep at it and see what I can find. But I'd get Abraham Wilberforce on this, if I were you.

"Just to be on the safe side."

Chapter Thirty-One

It wasn't until well into February that we had our first significant snow, more than a foot. I fired up my radiators that morning, put on an extra sweater, and settled in with coffee. As long as the power stayed on, I was good. If we lost power, I'd be fine with books and candles, until it got too cold. In that event, I could mush over to Ruth's. I imagined her huge fireplace would be a delight on a snowy winter day.

Our stub of a road filled with snow, and we waited. School was canceled, so no buses had to try to fight their way in to pick up Tina. Simeon had warned me that our piece of road was always the last to be plowed, and depending on weather and budgets, it could take a long time. So I had prepared, laying in a supply of canned and frozen foods, water, and plenty of coffee and wine.

That night, the temperature dropped. The moon was almost full again in a clear sky, and as I looked out my upstairs window, I could see the shadows of the branches twisted like veins across the blue-white ground.

Early the next morning, I pulled on boots and trudged down to the road. This time, I turned left, to where the road ended abruptly at the river. The cold had kept the snow from dropping off the bare branches, and they looked fluffy and feathery in the morning light.

I checked my watch. I'd been monitoring the ever-advancing time of sunrise over the winter, enjoying greeting it through my windows and observing how it inched back toward the north. This morning, sunrise was due right about…now.

And as if a light had been switched on, everything turned pink—the surface of the river, the mist, the clouds, and the snow-covered branches, which turned an intense pale rose, like cherry blossoms.

The whole world was pink. Like Renoir or Fragonard during their Pink Period. Like a Baroque chapel. Or someone's idea of heaven.

****

Because it was February, the temperature naturally changed daily. The next day it warmed up, and the snow on the trees plopped to the ground. Black patches appeared in the road, and Simeon got out his snow blower to clear tracks in the driveway. I had enjoyed the solitude of the last few days, but less than I usually did. I was restless, and I had much on my mind.

I went out my front door and through the thicket into the broad common driveway. The calendar said it was deep in winter, but the breezes spoke otherwise. There was a faint aroma of wood smoke in the air.

Tina, wearing a pink parka and a purple barrette in her hair, was playing with Camel, pulling a pine twig along and trying to get a reaction from him. But Camel was content to stay crouched in the sun, enjoying the entertainment provided by a little girl waving a branch in front of him.

"Hi, Tina. Are you and Camel enjoying this nice weather?"

She nodded, but without enthusiasm. "I want a

dog," she said, "but Mommy says she has enough to do, taking care of me, Nell, my dad, and the guests."

"That is a lot," I agreed, bending down to give Camel a pat between tan ears that looked as if they'd been chewed on at some point in his cat life.

"Maybe you could take care of the dog, when you're older." Melanie Butterfield might not appreciate my encouraging this particular project.

"I would," she said. "I take care of Nell. She can walk now."

"Really!" I realized the winter had gone by and I'd hardly seen my neighbors. "You must be proud of her!"

"Yeah." She appeared to have lost interest in Nell's accomplishments. "We go back to school tomorrow. I could have swarmed we'd go back today, because it isn't cold anymore."

"Well, I imagine they have to make sure the roads are clear enough for the buses."

Melanie approached with her coat unbuttoned and open. "Isn't this nice! And just in time. We're expecting two couples tomorrow for the weekend, so I have to get back to work, but Nell's napping, and it's so nice out here."

Her hands looked rough and chapped. From cleaning? Or did she wash the sheets on rocks down by the river? I asked what Paul did for a living, hoping my inner disapproval didn't come through.

"Oh, Paul is an artist," she said with a smile. "He's a poet, specifically. He teaches over at the community college and runs several workshops. But he needs time to think, and it's not easy to do that with two little girls." She smiled down at Tina and ruffled her taffy-colored hair. That loosened the barrette, so she bent down and refastened it.

Well, how nice, I thought. Can't have life and children interfering with the artist at work. Maybe Paul does lots of useful things in between stanzas. "Tina told me about her name," I said. "That's a wonderful tribute to his art, and to your daughter, as well."

"It is, isn't it?" Melanie's face glowed with pride. "And you know that Nelle's name is Villanelle?"

I confessed that I had not known that and wondered if I ought to admit that I wasn't sure what a villanelle was. I imagined it was a hard poem, as Tina had described the sestina.

"You know what it's like to write," Melanie said. "You can't do it while multitasking."

"Yes, but what I do doesn't use the same—what, brain waves?—as poetry. It's a lot more mechanical. And when I have everything in place—my interviews, my notes, my facts, and my lede, it's almost effortless."

We were silent for a while, enjoying the hints of spring to come. Melanie glanced back at her house. "This place was a dream of ours. Oh, I suppose the ultimate dream would be a bigger house, like that farm up the towpath. You've seen it, haven't you? If we had a place like that, we could serve our guests food we grew in our own gardens. I could make cheese from sheep's milk."

And offer horseback rides, and a petting zoo, hold poetry readings and have a few more babies, I thought. My admiration for Melanie and Paul was balanced by a sense of exhaustion.

****

By the end of February, the days grew perceptibly longer, but the temperatures dropped again.

I awoke one Tuesday morning and saw, as I looked out my eastern upstairs window, that the river had frozen. It wasn't solid, or full of huge icebergs, like the Ohio when Eliza fled Simon Legree. Some was in chunks like pieces of concrete broken up; some was just a submerged roughness, as if a herd of crocodiles were just under the surface. And everything moving, moving, left to right, the part closest to me moving more slowly, the whole thing looking as inexorable and destructive as a lava flow.

By Friday, the river cleared suddenly. Ominous weather reports told about an ice dam accumulating upriver. That put the upstream communities at risk for flooding and would threaten the downstream communities once the ice dam broke, which it inevitably would.

That afternoon, Marta knocked on my door and told me we might be evacuated if the river upstream rose any more. "They're saying the ice dam may break, and if that happens, the river will rise so fast no one will be able to get out in time," she said.

"How will we know?" I asked.

"Well, you and I are kind of on the border; I don't think our houses have ever flooded. But I would suggest you keep the radio tuned to 152 and pack an overnight bag. If anything happens, head up the hill to Ruth's. She's higher still, and I know her house is safe."

We heard crunching gravel, and turned to see a police car pulling in. A township officer got out and approached us.

"After tonight," he said, "if you go anywhere, it'll have to be by boat. Now's the time to leave, if you plan to.

"We're not actually ordering you to evacuate yet," he said, "because we don't think the water will get up this high. But you're almost sure to be cut off. Last time, the river and canal met in Yardley, and here, lots of you are going to be on islands."

He said a shelter had been set up in the high school for anyone who had to leave or wanted to.

"Have you decided what to do?" I asked Marta after he'd left to knock on Simeon's door.

"I'm staying," she said. "I'll be fine for a few days. Ruth is staying, of course, but the Butterfields are leaving. I'm not sure about Simeon."

But what should I do? Hole up? Head for the high school? Somehow, that didn't appeal. It was likely to be for one night, and I figured I'd manage. I looked up to my second floor windows and tried to imagine the Delaware reaching that high. No, I'd tough it out here.

And so I did. With help from the radio and the internet, I learned that the ice dam had broken around midnight, and the river rose rapidly. It was hard to see in the dark, but I could tell that it had crested its banks and was washing across the driveway. But the water never reached my threshold, and I stayed warm and dry on my own little island.

Next morning, I could tell that the water had receded a bit. I walked across my back yard, through the soaked grass, to the river. Usually it stayed settled between its banks, hidden from view unless you were close. I usually saw it most clearly from my upstairs windows.

But now, the water began at the edge of my yard, rather than down the banks. I could see a huge fibrous mass of branches and ice chunks strewn along the bank. The swollen river still carried branches, trash cans and outdoor furniture downstream.

A quick survey indicated that my neighbors had been spared any serious damage. Back inside, I checked traffic reports about road closings. As soon as I'd confirmed that River Road was open, I got in my car and went out to take a look.

The river had retreated, leaving angular boulders of ice marking its highest extent. Some were on the far side of the road, others up on the lawns of houses near the river bank. It looked as if everyone had dragged out their old white washing machines for trash pickup day.

On the banks, those trees that remained stood with their feet in the water, the bark on their north, or upriver, side, stripped off by ice, leaving stark white marks against the dark trunks, like a kind of negative moss.

Chapter Thirty-Two

Seth called. The Star and Garter had a flooded basement, but the sump pump was gaining on it.

He asked if he could come over and check out the river bank. He asked politely, as if he felt the need to tiptoe and not appear to be taking liberties with our new relationship.

When he arrived, we stood in the backyard and assessed the river. It had receded several more feet, but the rock where we'd had that difficult conversation a few months earlier was totally submerged. As if by mutual agreement, we avoided personal topics, and got down to business.

He started dragging tree limbs from the bank, along with oars, planks from someone's dock, and other flotsam. I helped him drag the debris down the driveway and to the street, where the trash people could figure out what to do with it.

Back at the river, Seth took one last look. I followed his gaze to a scrap of plywood wedged at the water's edge, against a steep part of the bank. It said, in rough painted letters, "rage Sale, 210 Coventry, L.M."

Recognition struck me. I'd seen this scrap floating upstream during the tidal bore. L.M. stood for Lower Morton, which was downstream from us. A sign for a garage sale, presumably.

Seth began yanking at the sodden panel. Some

vines tore away with it but remained stubbornly entangled with something. Seth bent to look more closely.

"Hey," he said. "This looks like some kind of door."

He pulled at something about the size of a garden gate, made of heavy wicker woven with wooden poles. I'd never seen it before and figured the scouring river had exposed it during the night.

It fell forward, revealing an opening in the bank. It was about the width of a standard door, but half as high.

"Man, I wish we had a flashlight," he said. I ran back into the house and grabbed the one I'd left on the kitchen counter in preparation for flood emergencies.

He was standing, waiting for me to come back. He took the torch and headed into the darkness. We crept inside a short, dank tunnel, away from the river.

Finally, another gate. There was no handle or anything to grip with to pull it open. He wedged his hands into the spaces between the sticks and pulled. The door came free, and Seth staggered back with it in his hands.

It was heavy. The other side of the door was faced with stone, regular shale blocks cut thin to reduce weight.

Seth dragged it to one side and bent into the space with the flashlight.

He was quiet for a while.

The suspense was getting to me. "Well?"

He laughed and pulled his head out. "That's a deep subject!"

"What?" This was becoming annoying. "What do you see?"

"It's a well. It must be the one in your backyard. It's dry, of course. Well, kind of muddy, but a dry well. Have a look."

He handed me the light and squeezed back behind me. I looked in. The base of the well had been filled in or used as a rubbish pit. Amid the dirt I could see shards of pottery and broken glass bottles. The stone sides, which extended only about eight or ten feet above us, were rough blocks of shale, like the outside of the well head in my back yard. Above, like a ceiling, was the concrete pad that covered it.

So that was why Ruth Lovering's well made that beautiful sound after a rain as water trickled in, and mine was silent. Of course. My water supply was from a newer well, and the original one, long dry, served no purpose.

At least it hadn't for the last hundred and fifty years or so.

"This has to have been a route to the river on the Underground Railroad," I said. "Ruth Lovering, up in the stone house, and her neighbor are convinced that her house was a stop, but they never found any sign. They must have held people in their house, then brought them over to my well when danger threatened, or when it was time to meet the boat that would take them across.

"That lid probably wasn't cement back then," Seth said. "Would it have been wood?"

"It was probably already an abandoned well, so it would have been covered with something safe but not easy to remove. Probably covered with vines and completely undetectable to bounty hunters.

"Let's get out of here," I said. I was growing

uncomfortable in the dark. I started to lead the way, carrying the torch.

"Wait!" Seth said. He was fingering a rock in the side of the well. I could see that it was set in loosely, without mortar. The stone was cut thin, like those facings on the wicker door. In the small space behind it was a small metal box, with a rubber band around it that secured an envelope.

I handed Seth the flashlight and carefully removed the envelope. It read:

CAUTION: TOXINS
Read before handling sample.

The note inside was hand written, and I recognized Elias' hand.

This box contains dormant spores of Lophodermium cf pinastri. *It is from a variety or sub-variety that may be toxic in humans if inhaled or ingested.*

I have preserved this sample for research purposes and stored it here where it is unlikely to be disturbed. If you find it, Do Not Open the box without following standard laboratory safety procedures.

It closed with the following:

This sample is from a section of the Humboldt National Forest in Humboldt County, Nevada. The source is a stand of Pinus contorta, and the specific location is detailed in accession book 27, dated September, 2010.

I carefully placed the box back in the niche.

We emerged into a brightness that seemed impossible on an overcast afternoon.

Chapter Thirty-Three

"I don't normally think of a Corolla as a cargo vehicle." I turned off the gravel driveway onto the road.

"Compared to my Mini, it is," Marta said, pulling on a pair of Fair Isle mittens. "I could have made two trips, but we should be able to fit all the fleeces in here, plus the trunk." She glanced into my backseat for confirmation. "Besides, this way, you can see the lambs."

The farm was only a few miles up the towpath, but farther by car. I drove along the main road and turned into the driveway. It crossed the canal and towpath, passed the stone house, and widened into a generous parking area near the barn and barnyard. We walked around to the front door and rapped the heavy wrought iron knocker against the oak door. I could see the pergola off to one side; to the other was the pasture, where I'd noticed the horses and sheep on my walks. The horses were out, wearing thick green blankets. The sheep were nowhere to be found.

A tall woman with lank, dark hair and deep-set brown eyes opened the door. She beamed at Marta and motioned us inside.

The entry was enormous, with a curving staircase disappearing into the upper shadows. A dark oval table nestled near the staircase, as if it had been made for the space. An explosion of yellow forsythia spilled from a cut crystal vase.

The woman turned to me and extended her hand. "I'm Sarah-Joy Renk." Without waiting to hear my name, she turned to Marta. "We were just about finished with lambing, but Fiona was late. She just dropped an hour ago, and Pablo is trying to get her into the barn."

We followed her through a vast, dark kitchen that gleamed metallically: copper, stainless steel, bronze in varying degrees of shine. Sarah-Joy wore a shapeless but expensive looking dress in a rough-textured linen, with a pattern of what looked like hand-printed sea creatures. She opened a side door and sent us off to the pasture.

We could see Fiona standing beyond temporary fencing that Pablo had set up to try to corral her into the barn. He was holding a small bundle wrapped in a yellow towel.

"Here," he said, handing the tiny lamb to me. For some reason, I welcomed the warm newborn; my aversion was gone. "Walk backward, facing her so she can see it."

I obeyed, and Fiona followed, bleating that familiar sheep sound that I remembered from my childhood. As we maneuvered through the final gate, Fiona grew confused, and momentarily lost track of her baby. Her bleating became desperate.

She charged back and forth, searching and bleating. Pablo grumbled.

Then the lamb in my arms squealed, and Fiona whirled toward the sound. She rushed through the gate and to my side. I held the lamb out toward her so she could nuzzle it and backed slowly into the barn. Marta quickly closed the gate behind her.

Soon we had Fiona and the baby in one of the small temporary stalls; on either side other ewes stood under heat lamps with their new lambs.

Pablo crouched next to Fiona and expressed colostrum from her udder into a bottle, a procedure he said stimulated lactation and saved the valuable nutrients for the lamb's first meal. Then he tagged her baby's ear, picked up a notebook, and wrote something in it.

Marta asked Pablo where she could find the fleeces, and Pablo, busy holding the bottle for the new lamb, motioned toward a stall at the far end of the barn. I was still enchanted by the lambs, but Marta had eyes only for the wool.

"Ah!" she exclaimed, moving forward to sink her hands into the clouds of cream, brown and black wool.

Marta selected four bundles, and Pablo slipped them into plastic bags for safe transit. He helped us carry them out to my car, and I waited while Marta went inside to pay Sarah-Joy.

I wanted to go back to the barn. Fiona's desperation had unnerved me, and I wanted to spend healing time with the reunited pair.

But Marta returned, and settled into the car with a bundle of ivory fleece on her lap. I drove down the gravel drive, over the towpath and canal, and out to the road.

"That's a beautiful house," I said, pulling onto the road. "What do you think of it, with your eye for interior spaces?"

"Oh, it's beautiful, all right. But it's only a reproduction. Only about five years old."

"What?" I jerked the steering wheel as I turned toward her. "A reproduction? But it looks so perfect!"

"A gazillion dollars buys a lot of perfect," she said. "The high ceilings, the huge kitchen, the convenient layout. People claim they want these authentic eighteenth-century houses, but most people don't have the fortitude to actually live in them. They're drafty and don't have any decent closets, and you're forever bumping your head on things."

I thought about that as we drove. The sun was slipping behind the woods along the road, filtering through a web of black branches.

"Ruth has fortitude," I said, as we approached the turnoff for Fenton's Crossing.

Marta nodded, from behind the wool. She seemed momentarily distracted as we passed the Star and Garter, but quickly turned her thoughts back to the discussion. "Thank goodness for people like Ruth, because without them, there wouldn't be any of the original houses left. There was a stone house on the Renks' property when they bought it, but they bulldozed it to make room for their grand mansion. That's what people do."

Marta's phone made a tweet sound, and she groped in her purse. She glanced at it just as we pulled into our driveway, then put it back.

We unloaded the car, carrying the fleece into her studio. She thanked me for the transportation, and I thanked her for the chance to see the lambs. As I pulled my car into my little yard, my mind was pulled back to the sheep again.

It was mid-afternoon, but my house seemed unusually dark.

Chapter Thirty-Four

We strolled through the Kingston campus. For once we weren't discussing fungi or research projects. We were just enjoying one another's company.

It was odd. When I was with Stephen, I felt alone. And I mean this in the best way. I felt the same tranquility, serenity, sense of safety, ability to allow my thoughts to unwind as they wished, that I did in my sanctuary of solitude. No demands, potential dangers, or even the fatigue that comes with social interactions.

We'd walked in silence for a long time when Stephen said, "You've never said much about your life before you came east, Miren. Is there a reason?"

It was probably time for my Explanation. Stephen seemed to be inching toward date territory recently. But I didn't quite know how to phrase it, what with all I'd learned about my changed past.

"You haven't mentioned your personal life either," I said. "Maybe we just haven't seen the need to share these things."

"Maybe not, so far. But unless you object, I'd like to tell you a bit about myself. What you do is your decision."

I was not unaccustomed to this, as I've said before. I usually end up knowing way more about other people than they know about me, and that's fine. So I said nothing.

"I got married in graduate school, probably unwisely, but we were in love. Nadezhda had immigrated from Russia with her family as a child. A beautiful dancer and a nerdy geneticist: Probably not a likely match."

"No more unlikely than many," I said, careful to avoid offering details from my own rich family history in that department.

"We were happy for quite a while, but after Anthony arrived, we both felt the stress. I was a post-doc, overwhelmed and underpaid. I tended to lose my temper over things I shouldn't. She was trying to get back in shape and prepare for auditions, while also taking on most of the baby care. We couldn't seem to stop needling each other.

"Eventually we realized we weren't being good to one another, or for one another. We separated but hesitated to divorce because of Anthony."

Still a fairly common tale, I thought, but kept quiet.

"Finally, she met someone else, and remarried. It works out okay. She's a good mother. Anthony likes his stepfather well enough. He lives with her, except on alternate weekends and for vacations as arranged."

"How old is he?"

Stephen shook his head gently, as if in awe. "He's ten now. He's a miracle to me."

I had a flashback to ten years ago, when I was noticing ten-year-old boys. I felt a moment of sorrow that I had never experienced Stephen's reverence for his child.

I quickly turned my thoughts to the revelations I was going to be expected to produce. I recognized the way people offer up intimate details of their own lives, in expectation of reciprocity. One of my colleagues in Reno was a master at this. She revealed carefully edited secrets, lulling her listener into a false sense of ease and camaraderie, which encouraged the listener to divulge secrets of her own. She acquired a lot of knowledge that she put to good use.

But I was a master, too. I knew how to keep my own counsel. I believe there are two ways to keep people from prying about sensitive personal issues. One is to refuse to say anything at all, which sometimes has the effect of attracting their interest like bait. The other is to offer rounded capsules of bland facts, so that the curious can fill up on what seems like real information but which, in fact, tells them little. With a little conversational jujitsu, you can get people happily talking about themselves again.

This is my preference, and the key is to polish those capsules smoothly, avoiding leaving loose threads that the inquisitive soul can grasp and tug.

But today, for reasons I don't fully understand, I grasped the loose thread myself.

"I guess I'd better tell you about Seth," I said.

"Seth?"

"He's someone I just met recently…"

Stephen's expression tightened a bit, as if he expected me to mention a lover. I made a note of that expression, and its implications, and filed it away.

"Seth is my son."

He looked at me as though I'd sprouted antlers.

"Your son? You never said anything about having a child."

"I didn't know I had a child."

He continued staring at the antlers. "You didn't

know? That's impossible…for a woman. Isn't it?"

And so I told him the story.

And after I told him the story back as far as Seth's birth, there was no way, really, not to tell him about what happened before.

****

When I was fifteen, my father died and my mother went crazy. I don't know if she went crazy from grief or if she was headed in that direction anyway, but she stopped functioning as the mother of a heartbroken teenager and went into some kind of early mid-life crisis.

She would disappear for days, and when she returned she'd corner me and talk excitedly about her adventures. She'd gone to Burning Man. She'd met a guru. She was investigating Scientology. At the time, I didn't think about practical things, like life insurance or how she was supporting us. I don't think she thought much about these things, either.

Then one morning she awakened me early and told me to pack a small suitcase, because we were going on an adventure. I was intrigued. She was taking me along! We loaded the truck and headed into the northern Nevada high desert.

The familiar landscape of Elk City fell away behind us. A few miles out, she dropped the bomb.

"I've remarried, and we're moving in with him."

The sky was getting lighter behind us. It reflected on the windshields of the occasional cars that passed us.

Finally, I was able to speak.

"But what about Dad?"

I was plenty old enough to understand that widows remarried. But it seemed so wrong, so impossible.

"Your father is dead, Miren. It's been almost a year. People do get married again."

I turned away and stared out the window. The scenery grew more desolate, and I sat silently, wondering what miserable cabin I was going to have to live in. I didn't even want to think about my friends, and the school paper, and everything I was leaving behind.

"I haven't been around much," she said. "This way, we'll be together. Things will be better."

We drove until midday, passing state wilderness areas and an Indian reservation. Finally, we turned onto an unpaved road, its surface white and dusty.

The road turned and ran along a high, rusty chain-link fence. We stopped at a gate and my mother got out to open it. We drove through, and I got out and closed it. Westerners do this by rote; you never leave a gate open behind you.

After another mile, a group of prefab houses appeared. Several were fairly attractive, with porches and shutters. Others were trailers mounted on cinder blocks. We pulled in next to several trucks and a Bobcat utility vehicle. I could tell by the way she maneuvered the truck that she'd been here before.

Two women came out to greet us. They wore faded cotton house dresses with their hair in braids tied up over their heads. They greeted my mother warmly and did a quick assessment of me. The one who introduced herself as Sister Barbara took me to one of the outbuildings. Inside was a large room with bunk beds, and a bathroom. She gestured to one of the lower bunks, and I set my suitcase on it. It was like the first day at camp, when nothing looks familiar and you're convinced that nothing ever will. She told me where the main building was, said she'd see me at dinner, and left.

That evening, as we assembled in the dining room for a communal supper, I met my stepfather.

He was lean and tough-looking, what my mother's family referred to as "wiry." He had pale blue eyes. Not all blue eyes look cold, but his did.

My mother introduced him as Elder Morrow. He looked at me with great intensity and introduced the women who'd met us as his wives. At first, I thought he meant that they were ex-wives, but it soon dawned on me that my mother was just one of three.

We sat down, and Elder Morrow led grace. It was like no grace I'd ever heard, and I've heard many. There was talk of Biblical prophecy, of retribution and tribulation, of smiting. Very little about food, and nothing at all about gratitude.

Over the next few weeks, we fell into a routine. My mother worked in the office, composing press releases and lists of demands, and assisting a lawyer who dropped in occasionally to handle the many sticky legal issues that the compound generated.

I was assigned the task of teaching the younger children to read, which I didn't actually mind. I hated my situation, but I was able to lose myself in the process of helping small children make sense of the marks on a page. Nobody said anything more about homeschooling me.

Then, a few months after I turned sixteen, Elder Morrow summoned me to his office. I stood before him as he sat at his wooden desk.

"I've been watching you as you work with the children, Miren. You perform your duties well."

I stood silently.

"Now it's time for you to assume a greater role. The Lord has plans for you. For us. He has ordered me to take you as my wife."

As I so often did, I spoke carelessly. "Don't you have a wife? Um, wives?"

He smiled slightly.

"You're sixteen now. It's time."

My mouthy impulse welled up again, but this time I asked my questions silently. If I don't want to, it isn't a real marriage, right? What about my own mother? I won't do it!

He saw my thoughts through the silence. He moved several file folders from one side of the desk to the other and stood up.

"It's settled," he said.

We were married, if you can call it that, by a traveling clergyman (or pseudo clergyman) who said a lot about fulfilling prophecies and the usual references to smiting and tribulation. After a simple wedding feast, my new husband took me to his room.

I tried not to look at him. He made me. His eyes were burning, but still cold blue. He undressed me. He left the light on. He'd worn a dark suit for the wedding, and he laid the jacket neatly on a chair. He unbuttoned his shirt with one hand, pulling on the buttons until I thought they'd break off. When he was undressed, I could see the contrast between his weathered, tanned face and hands, and a pale, vulnerable body that looked as if it belonged to a different creature.

Then he was on top of me, hurting me. I didn't have to look at his eyes anymore.

Afterward, he fell asleep. I did not. Then he awoke,

235

and was on top of me again. It hurt worse than the first time, but the next night, and every night after that, I felt nothing at all.

My mother stopped speaking to me. I couldn't ask her why I felt so tired, why the slightest odor would make me queasy. When I began to show, she disappeared. I never saw her again.

As the pregnancy progressed, I lost the will to escape. I grew very large, and very tired, with swollen ankles and all manner of aches and pains. I thought vaguely about what it might be like to give birth in a non-hospital setting, but—being naturally naïve—I figured, well, pioneer women, and women for millions of years, have been doing this, so I probably could, too.

As it happened, I survived, but my baby did not— as also happened to pioneer women and generations of women before them.

But it was survival on a very basal level. I was alive, still bleeding, still in pain. It hurt when I got up, and it hurt when I sat down. My breasts hurt when they tried to make milk for a baby who wasn't there. All I could think about was being somewhere else. I couldn't stay.

I waited until after dark, when Sister Barbara and Sister Anne had checked on me and believed I was asleep. I left the compound, unsteady on my feet. When I reached the chain-link fence, I managed to fit the toe of my shoe into the link, but I was too weak to lift myself. I followed the fence around the perimeter of the property until, finally, I found a gap, probably made by animals. I squeezed through and started down the gravel road.

It was November and bitter cold after the sun had

gone down. I walked along the dirt road, ready to bolt for the thin underbrush if I heard one of the compound vehicles pursuing me. I finally made it to the highway.

It was nearly dawn when a sheep truck came by and stopped. Shivering, I told the driver I had to get away from my husband and begged him for a ride.

He took me to a truck stop, handed me twenty dollars, wished me luck, and headed off.

The route from that truck stop to the newspaper in Reno was long and rough. I don't quite know why I decided to make the move to Bucks County, but part of it was that I'd had just about enough of Nevada.

****

We'd been walking along paths through the campus and hadn't been paying attention to where we were. I looked up and saw the Gothic façade of the Chapel, rising from the cold ground. Stephen had been silent during my recitation.

"I've managed pretty well since then, but there are a few aspects of my life that aren't conventional," I said. "One, of course, is that I have a mother somewhere and haven't exactly figured out what I think about her. She's not like most people's mothers."

Stephen nodded and remained silent.

"Another is that I have no…capacity for relationships with men. The idea of a physical relationship is traumatic.

"And, of course, now I have a son I never knew I had. As you probably have guessed, there two babies. It's a miracle that the second one survived, but he did."

Stephen had moved closer to me. He seemed to want to touch me, in a comforting way. A shoulder pat, a touch of the hand. But he was too smart for that. It would not have been a good idea.

We reached his car, and he lifted the hatch to put his camera bag away.

He rolled back the cargo cover and placed the camera on a folded orange windbreaker. It was a fairly common windbreaker, but I knew I had seen it before. On a man who looked like Stephen. From above. Hastily leaving the Mercer Museum.

We drove home in silence, and I'm sure Stephen was thinking about what I'd told him. I was thinking about the windbreaker.

And people with volatile tempers.

And Accession Book No. Twenty-Seven, which was among the notebooks Stephen had borrowed.

Chapter Thirty-Five

It was early March, with a hint of spring in the air. Seth and I had taken lawn chairs out to the side of the yard with a river view.

We had confirmed our biological relationship with GenomTech and were adjusting to our new realities. We had agreed that, for the time being, at least, we would treat each other as friends.

When I had searched the company's website, checking out how to use their kit to collect and mail cheek swabs, I had glanced at the list of Frequently Asked Questions, and had seen one that stopped me in my tracks:

"Is it possible to obtain a good DNA sample from a toothbrush?"

The answer was, yes, but proper cheek swabs are likely to provide a clearer match.

I asked him point blank. "Did you steal my toothbrush?"

He seemed surprised by the question. Then blushed.

"We hadn't even met then," he said, "and I didn't think you were going to be cool with the idea."

"Well, you thought right. That doesn't seem a bit sneaky to you?"

"Yeah, I suppose it does. I suppose picking someone's lock and getting into their house is a bit sneaky, too. But you have to admit I'm honest."

"We'll see," I said, grumpily.

Even when we were at odds, I felt comfortable in his presence. We watched the river, and I thought about my bad years and how they served to excuse me and my shortcomings and oddities. I'd locked those experiences away, and thought I'd neatly sealed them off, but they controlled me from their cold prison.

Yet Seth had experienced more than a few bad years of his own. Unlike me, he'd never had a stable home, loving if imperfect parents, and the sense of people who put a premium on his well-being.

And yet, here he was, sane, reasonable, open. Or so he appeared. Was I overlooking something, some scar tissue in his personality? Had he been more damaged than I suspected?

My feelings ranged from annoyance to bewilderment, guilt, and wonderment. Some days I wanted him out of my life; I wanted my old life back, such as it was. Other days I found myself missing him, his even disposition, the way he seemed grounded despite everything. And he was considerate of my feelings now, although he certainly hadn't been during his stalking and housebreaking stage.

Seth had asked me about my parents, his grandparents. I told him what I knew. I thought of telling him about the letters, currently in the hands of the appraiser in New Hope, but hesitated. I was planning to give Seth the letters with a Lassiter connection someday but decided not to mention them yet.

After a while, I asked him something that had been on my mind. "Now that you've found me, what do you want? You've spent a major part of your life looking for me. Have you thought about what happens next? Have you ever thought beyond your search?"

He shifted in his chair and was quiet for a while. Then he spoke. "Do you want to know what you're like?"

He saw my look of confusion and laughed quietly.

"I'll tell you. You are angelic. You have wavy blond hair and blue eyes and a kind face. You've been looking for me for twenty years. You wept with joy when we found each other. You baked me cookies. You're small, and vulnerable. You need someone to look out for you. To protect you."

Without thinking, I laughed. I was afraid I had offended Seth, but a smile played on his lips as well. I thought about his decades of wondering about his mother. I wondered if Sister Barbara had told him idealized stories about me, or if they had spoken of me at all. I filed those questions away for later.

"So I must be something of a disappointment." I said.

He was quiet for a moment, and I felt embarrassed, as though my comment was fishing for some kind of compliment. "I have to get used to the real you," he said. "And I have to say, there's stuff I like."

I said, "There's stuff I like in the real you, too. But I never had an imaginary you to compare it with."

Seth had his hands in his coat pocket and jingled what sounded like his keys but were probably his lock-picks. "I'd like to get to know you as a friend, if that's possible," he said. "I don't want to do some kind of fake mother-son reunion, because even if that's what's happening, it can't really be how we feel. Yet."

There were so many questions. Would he enroll in college? Would he be able to afford it? Were there weird scholarships dedicated to kids born on polygamous compounds to mothers who don't know they exist? And what would he study? What had he studied during his brief time at community college? What were his strengths and interests? His dreams? I decided to be patient and file these questions along with the others I was collecting to ask later.

As it happened, Seth had a question of his own.

"Do you have a doctor?"

I wasn't expecting that. "Not really. Why do you ask?"

"Because you really should. You shouldn't just go on and on, without even a check-up. Especially a woman."

I sat back in my chair and looked at him in amazement. "What's this all about?"

He didn't respond, so I said, "For your information, I don't get sick. I don't need anything related to birth control, not that it's the least bit your business. Okay?

After a brief silence, I added, "And I have an aversion to being examined. I guess you could call it a phobia, if you insist."

"You have good reason," he said. "But I still think it's important that you take care of yourself."

"Apparently that's not necessary. Everybody else seems to be doing a fine job of that for me." I thought about Simeon's mother-hen behavior, and Marta's concern about my aesthetic life.

I gave him a sharp look. "What about you? Do you go to doctors all the time?"

"That's different. I'm only twenty-one, and I'm a

guy."

He said it in a dismissive tone, as though it was a foolish question. I countered that he was the one who'd brought the subject up.

We'd been mother and son for less than a week, and here we were arguing and nitpicking. I wondered if I could send him to his room or ground him. I had no idea how any of that even worked.

Chapter Thirty-Six

A few days later, I noticed I'd missed a call on my cell. The number matched the one on the card Detective Parnell had given me at our last meeting. I remembered my conversation with Spencer and was glad I hadn't heard the call. I needed time to think.

That afternoon, I got an email from someone who identified himself as Joseph Whitacre, a member of the Cooperville Historical Society and a friend of the late Graham Farnsworth. His organization had long been interested in efforts to preserve or develop the Wintergreen Estate, at the center of the juvenile court scandal. According to Whitacre, title had never actually transferred from the previous owners, a disputatious family, to Bennington, the prison developer.

The Historical Society still had the right of access to the property for research purposes. Because of its uncertain future, Whitacre wanted the *Clarion* to tell the property's story. He said he was most easily reached by email.

I sent a text to Jodi to see if there was any interest, and if so, whether I should be the one to do the story. It related to Mark's series, but it seemed like more of a feature, a tour of the property and an interview with an expert on its history. She texted back with the go-ahead, and I sent Whitacre a response.

He got back to me almost immediately, and

suggested Tuesday at four p.m. He planned to leave work a bit early so there would still be some light while we explored the property.

Tuesday afternoon, I called Mark to make the same backup arrangement that had saved his life. He said he was tied up, so he transferred me to Spencer.

Spencer was happy to help. I told him where I'd be and asked him to give me a call around five. I couldn't imagine that a devoted local preservationist would have an evil streak, but after everything that had been going on, I wasn't going to meet anyone in a haunted house without backup.

After everything was arranged, I arrived at the Wintergreen property. Even though Whitacre had invited me, I wanted to avoid any appearance of trespassing, so I parked on Sullivan Road and walked down to where the weedy gravel driveway led to the vine-covered façade of the mansion. In summer, this property would be completely obscured, but in late winter, it was easy to see how sadly ramshackle it was. First floor windows were boarded up, but some second floor and attic panes were missing, suggesting dreadful water damage to floors and walls. Leaning wooden columns tried to support what remained of a wooden porch roof over the main door. It sagged lopsidedly, as did the few shutters that remained. In the distance I could see the ruins of a stone barn.

I knocked at what I thought was the front door. A paper note taped to the wooden panels read:

Miren,

No doorbell. Come in. I'm in the hall (first floor, to your left)

J.W.

I pushed the door open with a creak and stepped inside.

Before me was a wide entry hall floored with large checkerboard tiles, black and possibly white, although it was hard to tell under the ancient grime. To the right rose a dark staircase, with carved balusters and a wide banister that ended in a graceful scroll. Presumably, the hall was a large room off this entrance area.

Toward the back and on the left, I made out an open doorway with a heavy brown curtain hanging on rings over it. It must, at one time, have been an elegant velvet, but it was in tatters now.

I slid back the curtain.

And there stood Lawrence.

Chapter Thirty-Seven

I exhaled. "Lawrence. Jeesh. You scared me to death. What are you doing here?"

He smiled. I briefly considered that he might be a member of the Cooperville Historical Society, sharing a passion for vintage treasures and working side by side with Whitacre.

But not for long.

The room resembled Ruth's keeping room, probably an original wing of the house that predated the elegant addition. An enormous fireplace, larger than Ruth's, dominated the far end. A wave-front dresser stood against the wall, with one drawer missing.

Lawrence's sunglasses, a water bottle, and an envelope lay in the dust on the dresser top, along with an unlit oil lamp, a length of rope coiled like a snake, and something metallic that I couldn't make out in the fading afternoon light. I could see glassware, old-style test tubes set in some kind of rack, and copper or bronze coils above. What looked like Elias' vintage balance sat next to the apparatus.

The light was fading, but I could still see his eyes. They were the cold kind of blue. Benjamin Morrow blue.

"Where is Joseph Whitacre?" I asked.

Lawrence smiled again. "Sadly, there is no Joseph Whitacre. There should be, don't you think?" He looked appraisingly around the room. "It's a fascinating place."

Keeping those blue eyes on me, he edged over to the dresser and picked up the metal object. It was a syringe, the old-fashioned kind with round rings for the fingers. The needle was thick and ugly.

"It's really quite amazing," he said. "You hold in your hands the capacity to end a life, or many lives, as you see fit. And there are no consequences. No detectable cause of death; strictly natural. Starvation, or, before that, dehydration.

"It's even merciful," he said, his voice almost tender, "which is important to me. People shouldn't suffer. Even if they appropriate my father's work. Even if they angle to cut me out of the benefits of a discovery my father made. Even if they refuse to share the precious material that would be worthless without my father's contribution.

"My father was an intellectual giant, you know. Your uncle? He was losing his edge, Miren. He was beginning to do absent-minded things. He hid an important letter in the instruction manual of a drying oven. Can you imagine? Losing his edge.

"And that reporter! Threatening to accuse me in the newspaper. Or that historian! Cornering me in a museum and threatening me with arrest. Calling me a vandal." He laughed wryly and shook his head vigorously. "I am not a vandal."

"What are you, then?" I asked quietly, wondering what time it was.

He paused and looked to the side, as if in thought. "I am a man who has never been given the respect he deserves. Whose genius has always been dismissed.

Whose knowledge has always been ignored by ordinary people. A man who will, eventually, receive what is rightfully his."

He moved toward me.

"You won't feel a thing," he said, almost regretfully. "You'll lose consciousness, and that will be that. This property is in limbo. No one will get around to inspecting it for months. You may someday be found, but no one will be able to determine a cause of death.

He held up the syringe.

I stepped back and planted my feet slightly apart, one in front of the other. I crouched, holding my arms in front of me, bouncing lightly on my toes. It was a wrestling stance; I'd seen Jason use it in high school. I hoped it made me look stronger than I was.

He smiled and set the syringe aside.

He reached for the rope instead.

He cornered me near the fireplace and grabbed my wrists. I struggled, but he was strong. Really strong. My hands were behind me, tightly knotted. I kicked at him, but he deftly twisted out of my way. He couldn't cut the thick rope, but started to bind the other end around my ankles. He began to make a knot.

My phone rang.

He grabbed my purse and shook it upside down. Pens, Chapstick, a small reporter's notebook, tissues, car keys, and the phone rained down on the floor and rolled or drifted under furniture. He cursed. He made a dive for the phone, but by the time he picked it up, it was silent. He slipped it into his pocket.

I was seated against the fireplace wall, with my knees drawn up but unbound. I wondered how much fighting I could do with legs only. Somehow, I had to keep that syringe away.

He began putting things back in the purse, for what reason I couldn't imagine. Tidiness seemed inappropriate at a time like this. He paused and set the purse down, reaching to move the oil lamp closer along the top of the chest.

He removed the globe and turned the knob that raised the wick. He picked up a book of matches, and soon a blue flame flared, then settled into a warm glow. He carefully replaced the globe. The pool of light from the lamp made the rest of the room seem darker.

He did a final search in the area of brightness, apparently looking for anything he might have missed.

Finally, he picked up the syringe.

He came toward me.

Suddenly he stopped, listening. I heard it, too. Gravel crunching under tires.

Lawrence cursed again and headed out of the room toward the front door. I wondered what kind of story he'd tell Spencer, and whether it would succeed.

I screamed Spencer's name as loud as I could, but I doubted he'd hear me. I needed to stand up and get out while I could.

The rope around my ankles wasn't actually knotted, but my hands were helpless behind my back. I tried to unwind the rope by thrashing my legs. I rolled and twisted, until my back was against the stone fireplace surround.

And then, as fate would have it, I was snagged. Of course. The rope had hooked onto something, binding me to the stone. I fought off panic and pulled forward, writhing from side to side to try to free the rope from whatever it had caught on.

Suddenly I heard a gritty sound, stone moving against stone. I had caught the knot around my wrists on something sharp on one of the stones on the flank of the huge fireplace.

Iron hooks are hardly surprising accessories in these old fireplaces, but a movable stone was. I tried leaning carefully forward.

Slowly, slowly, the stone, and several others it was attached to, moved out like a very small door.

The rope fell away from the hook. I squeezed into the space and used the inside handle on the door to pull it closed with my feet.

Like the people before me who might have hidden here on their way to freedom, I listened intently to what was going on outside. Sounds were muffled by the stones, but I thought I heard the same crunching sound I'd heard before—a car. Was Spencer leaving?

The front door slammed, and I heard approaching footsteps.

Lawrence?

Spencer?

Then I heard Lawrence's voice.

It had a gentle, beseeching sound. Almost hoarse.

He called my name several times, his voice rising toward panic.

I could hear his feet thumping on the floorboards as he ran around the room, searching for someone who clearly wasn't there. What had he told Spencer?

The footsteps retreated and I heard the front door again. He was probably racing around the perimeter of the house, tripping over the underbrush in the twilight, trying to head off my escape.

He was gone a long time. I imagined him with a flashlight, sweeping the light across the overgrown brambles and leafless vines. I remembered I'd parked my car on Sullivan Drive, at the edge of the property. Would he remember it was mine? Would he disable it somehow? I tried to remember if he'd ever actually seen my car.

Even so, I had no car keys. If I could get free, I'd have to make a run for it. I thought about crawling out and trying to escape without the use of my hands, but I was afraid I'd just fall down and be easy pickings. My hiding place was at least safe.

He must be desperate. After his revelations, he couldn't let me go. What was he thinking? What was his plan?

What was mine?

I went back to work on the knots. It might take hours, but it appeared that I had time on my side.

And finally, the rope fell away. My hands were free.

Now what?

Where was Lawrence?

It might be best to stay in my priest hole as long as it took to outwait him. But how long would that be?

I'm quite sure I dozed. Horrible as my dark prison was, I was afraid to leave. I was exhausted, and thirsty. I leaned against the stone door and slowly, slowly, opened it an inch. Two inches. The room seemed bathed in light, like a brightly lit stage. But it was only the oil lamp sputtering now with its last fuel. I'd been in total darkness so long it seemed like high noon.

Something gleamed on the floor, under the window sill. My eyes picked it up immediately: my car keys.

Lawrence had somehow missed them when he put things back in my purse, which I didn't see anywhere. Should I grab the keys and make a dash for my car? What if he'd slashed my tires? What if he was waiting outside the front door? What would he do, given my mystifying disappearance?

Should I wait in my hiding place until daybreak? No; if he was still on the property, I'd stand a better chance of escape in the dark. I took a breath and pushed the door open.

Nothing.

I crept toward the keys, as silently as I could. It was slow going, since my body was tight and cramped from its long confinement. I reached the keys and grabbed them by the blades to avoid jingling.

Nothing.

I made my way to the front door and cracked it just enough to look outside. All I could see was darkness. I slipped out.

Nothing.

I stumbled several times as I made my way across the dark, tangled yard toward the car. It appeared undamaged. Lawrence must not have recognized it as mine. I scrambled through my memories and concluded that Lawrence had never actually seen my car.

No time to inspect the tires. I grabbed the door handle and cursed silently as the dome light came on when the door opened. I hurled myself in, locked the doors and started up.

I left my headlights off and coasted down Sullivan toward the main road. Then I switched the lights on as I pulled onto the highway.

Stupid!

Because as I did so, I saw another car's lights flash on in the woods behind me.

Lawrence?

It would have to be. Who else could it be? I darted a glance to my dashboard clock. It was nearly six a.m. We'd been there all night.

I sped down the dark streets, heading for—where? The police station? Who would be there at this hour? The whole county used dispatchers in the off-hours, buried in some hidden office in Doylestown. No stores were reliably open at this hour. I would never make it to some stranger's porch and persuade them to rescue me in time.

Surely my best bet was to lose him. I headed out of town, onto the back roads I'd become so familiar with. It was a clear night; I could see the stars above the dark tree line.

His lights stayed with me.

I hurtled along Van Sant road and onto the covered bridge. My tires rumbled. The headlights lit up the wooden interior like a rustic ski lodge.

On the other side, I kept an eye on headlights behind me, which I had to assume were Lawrence's.

In the rearview mirror, I saw the flare of light within the bridge, and estimated he was no more than two minutes behind me.

And closing in.

Now the dashboard clock said 6:10. Something made me remember the room where Lawrence had waited for me. The dresser, with its layer of dust, leaves, desiccated insects. The thick envelope, the water bottle. His sunglasses. I couldn't remember if the hypodermic was still on the table when I left.

I estimated the time it would take me to get where I needed to be. I tried to recall the angle of the sun at daybreak. I did a mental MapQuest.

I slowed down a bit, to make sure Lawrence was close enough behind me so he could see where I turned. I led him for several miles past fields and woods and darkened houses.

The sky was growing lighter, faintly. But it was still dark enough that my headlights picked up Rogers Brothers produce stand, the new synagogue, a cornfield bristling with stubble. The clock said 6:16. I adjusted my speed carefully. We had to hit the straight section at exactly 6:18. To the southeast was the stand of tall maples I'd observed many times, in different seasons. Now they stood bare, parallel dark lines against the peach-colored south-eastern sky.

The image of Lawrence's sunglasses hovered in my mind, and I pulled him behind me as if I were towing him on a rope.

The sun burst above the horizon, as bright as it had ever been. My eyes, accustomed to the darkness, snapped into a squint. The light flashed through the trees at an angle, flickering as I drove, bright-dark, bright-dark, like the barcode scanner in a supermarket.

In the new brightness, my mirror showed me the gray Citroën, buglike as it raced along behind me. At first it seemed to slow down, pulling farther back from me. And then it twisted, as though spinning on a patch of ice, but there was no ice. It spun again, tilted off the road, flipped once, twice, until it folded around a tree. The last thing I saw in the mirror was the front left tire, spinning counterclockwise, more and more slowly, in the bright morning air.

Chapter Thirty-Eight

My neighbors and I gathered in Paul and Melanie's living room, cramped because we were all there. All except Ruth Lovering, who wouldn't be joining us. Lawrence was her relative, and she was grieving with family.

Simeon held Nelle on his lap. Jim and Ellen Bollinger sat next to him, Roberta Jennings stood, and Marta sat close to Desmond on the settee. Seth and I sat on spindle-back chairs, while Paul perched on the bottom step of the stairs as Melanie moved back and forth from the kitchen with coffee.

I nodded and picked up my coffee. My thoughts flicked to Lawrence and his opinions about Potlatch.

"I owe you all an explanation, and now that everything finally makes sense, I can give you one. It's easier to tell you all together, rather than one at a time."

I began with the break-ins, the theft of my toothbrush, and the discovery in the well. I confessed that at times I'd suspected villagers, along with the Kingston people. I explained that because of what I'd learned, the police were reviewing my uncle's death as a possible homicide and had rejected the anonymous tip implicating me in the attack on Mark. I explained how Lawrence was most likely the anonymous informant. How he must have had access to a limited amount of the fatal fungus from his father's supply, and that he wanted more. I explained what happened at the Wintergreen mansion, and how I'd hidden and made my getaway.

I turned to Roberta Jennings. "I owe everything to you, Roberta. The Underground Railroad saved my life."

She nodded solemnly. "The latest of many," she said. "You're in esteemed company."

I turned to Seth and said quietly, "Are you sure about this?"

He nodded. "I am if you are."

I resumed. "Finally, I want to introduce a family member. This is my son, Seth Morrow. Why I never mentioned him before is, well, a long story."

Seth acknowledged the group's greetings graciously, but I thought I saw a faint blush under the scraggly beard. For a moment, I wanted the beard to go away. Not by shaving, but by a rewinding of time, a rewinding of the man into the boy I'd never known.

****

The police had found my phone on Lawrence's body, and returned it to me. That was good, because I needed to talk to Stephen. I'd left several messages, and hadn't heard back. Finally, I called the department.

"Hi, Mia. This is Miren. I'm trying to get in touch with Stephen."

"So are we," she said. "We haven't seen him in almost a week."

"Oh," I said. I didn't want to pry, but Mia's voice carried a note of concern. "Is this something he does on occasion? Could he have gone somewhere with his son?"

"Not without letting us know," she said. "I've

called his house and left messages on his landline. But nothing."

We agreed we'd let each other know if either of us heard anything.

No sooner had I hung up than the phone rang. I was hoping for Stephen, but it was Spencer.

"Miren! F.X. just told us. I'm going to be writing the police aspect of this. And the Farnsworth case...well, this changes a lot. But I just found out you were there all along, at Wintergreen. What happened?"

"I was there, all right. Was that you? Why did you leave?"

"I called, you know. You didn't pick up, so I came right over. Lawrence met me, and said you'd gotten a phone call and left in a hurry. I believed him. I thought you weren't there.

"I only met Lawrence that once, at Krakatoa with Mark." Spencer said. "I thought he was your boyfriend."

I shuddered.

"He wasn't, I can assure you. But thanks for coming, anyway, Spence."

"Oh, and you know what else was strange? He called me Mark."

At Krakatoa, my introductions had been hasty. And Spencer had picked up Mark's coffee order when the barista called it out. Lawrence must have gotten the two reporters mixed up, thought Mark was zeroing in on the Farnsworth investigation, and acted murderously on that misunderstanding.

****

Seth and I sat at the bar at the Star and Garter. I was drinking Harp, and Seth had poured himself a soda.

258

Seth asked, "So Lawrence tried to kill you because you knew about his other attempts?"

"They weren't just attempts. He killed my uncle. That fall in the storeroom wasn't an accident. It's true that my uncle died of dehydration, but Lawrence set it up. The same thing would have happened to me, and to Mark."

Seth rattled the ice cubes in his drink. "I can see Lawrence being resentful about a colleague, like your uncle. And feeling threatened by someone who seemed to be putting all the pieces together, like you. But what reason would he have to attack Mark?"

"That was all a mistake," I said. "He was concerned about the stories Spencer was writing about Graham Farnsworth's death. When we met at Krakatoa, I introduced them in a way that made Lawrence think Mark was his enemy."

Seth snorted. "You really shouldn't try to kill someone unless you're sure you have the right guy," he said. "But even so, what motivated him in the first place?"

"I don't think we'll ever know," I said, moving my glass around the bar top to make interconnected rings. "All I know is that he had some sort of—I don't know, narcissism? I sensed it during our conversations but didn't really pick up on it. He was so intelligent, but now, in retrospect, I realize there was something missing inside."

We sat quietly for a while. I realized with searing clarity what a hollow man Lawrence was. What seemed like ordinary insecurity was really something much deeper—or shallower. All Lawrence's efforts to bolster his self image, and to separate the world into unworthy lesser beings and a few admirable worthies like himself, were strategies designed to protect the frail vulnerability of the inner Lawrence.

When I was in first grade, we did a craft project that involved blowing up balloons, draping them with string soaked in glue, and creating a lattice that bore the shape of our balloons. When the string dried, we had the fun of popping the balloons, and made the remaining string lattice into lanterns. An ornate, precisely constructed shell, concealing inside itself—nothing.

"I honestly don't think he saw the evil in what he was doing. He didn't see other people as people. He saw them as objects, and it was perfectly okay, in his mind, to move them around to suit him. Or remove them, if necessary."

Something in my brain lurched.

I stood so abruptly I almost overturned the stool.

"Oh my god. Where does Stephen live?"

I called Mia, who gave me his address in West Windsor, in New Jersey. "But I don't know how you'll get in," she said.

"Call the police to do a welfare check. I can get in," I said. I disconnected, grabbed Seth, and headed for my car.

****

Stephen lived in a nondescript townhouse in a pleasant but bland development. It took us seemingly forever to find his unit.

I banged on the door. After all, it was possible, barely, that he was fine, and had his own reasons for not communicating.

There was no response. Seth pulled out his tools,

knelt in front of the door, and got to work.

My brain disconnected briefly as I watched him. His hands moved with the assurance of a surgeon. The urgency of the situation didn't make him rush.

Finally, I heard a distinct click, and Seth pushed the door open.

We were met with the unmistakable odor of catastrophe. Not death, necessarily, but of someone unattended and dying.

Stephen was lying on the living room carpet, his clothing stained, his skin a pallid yellow. His face on its side looked shrunken, skull-like.

But his chest moved. He was alive.

I called 911. If this was Lawrence's doing, he had to have assaulted Stephen before me, and that was nearly a week ago.

Seth found a blanket and we covered him. I remembered from first aid not to give liquids to an unconscious victim, but I worried about how dehydrated he was. The seconds and minutes passed agonizingly as we waited for the ambulance.

****

As soon as Stephen was safely under treatment, we began checking on everyone we could think of who had crossed Lawrence's path, anyone he might have had a grudge against and who might be lying under a haystack somewhere. Everyone was accounted for.

It wasn't until the next day that I was allowed to see Stephen. He was hooked up to an IV and looking much better. He told me that the last thing he remembered was seeing Lawrence at his front door.

I told him how we'd found him and brought him up-to-date on everything that he had missed. I told him about my adventure at Wintergreen Hall, and about Lawrence's death. I told him about finding the fungus sample in the well, something I hadn't had a chance to mention before.

Finally, I had a question that had been on my mind. "What were you doing at the Mercer Museum the day Graham Farnsworth was killed?"

He looked surprised at my question. A crinkle developed between his eyebrows.

"How did you know I was there?" he asked.

"I'd seen someone who looked like you leaving the Mercer in an orange windbreaker, just after we'd found Graham Farnsworth's body—before they closed the museum and sent everyone out."

He nodded thoughtfully. "My son had a school trip that morning that I had agreed to chaperone. A trip that, I might add, was canceled, to his great disappointment. I'd gone early to get a preview. I thought it would be more fun for all of us that way.

"I went out to the parking lot to meet the bus. By the time they unloaded the kids, word had come that the museum was closed. They were vague about why, so we didn't stress out too much. We went to the Moravian Pottery and Tile Works instead, which was okay but less fun for ten-year-olds.

"Miren, did you suspect me? Did you really think I went around stabbing people with fungus? Letting them die?"

"There was a lot we didn't know about each other until recently," I said. "I didn't know who to trust. And it spooked me when I saw the same windbreaker in your trunk last week."

We sat in comfortable silence for several minutes.

Then I spoke again.

"Did you ever take Anthony to the museum?"

"No. I should—when I get out of here. Maybe you'd like to join us."

Chapter Thirty-Nine

Jodi kept me on the phone for what seemed like hours. She explained the story she wanted me to write. She expressed horror and sympathy for my ordeal. She took time to update me on happenings in the newsroom.

June Snodgrass had announced her retirement. Carlos, the courthouse reporter, was leaving to cover the Montgomery County courts for another paper. Ezra Blum had been offered his position and was thrilled to get out of sports at last.

"Oh, and Miren! Guess what? Pradip is engaged."

"That's great," I said. "So I guess the matchmaking aunt found someone suitable to all parties?"

"Hardly," said Jodi. "He's engaged to Jen."

Jen? The meek obituary writer from Levittown? And Pradip? The handsome IT expert from West Bengal? It just might work, I thought. Stranger things have.

"Oh dear," I said.

"Oh dear is right. Apparently there was quite an uproar over in Kolkata. But Pradip insists everything will be fine, and that once the doubters meet Jen, all will be well."

We hung up, and I set to work mapping out my story. For this one, I had no notes, but an outline would be essential.

I remembered there was plain paper in the flat

drawer in the typing table. As I rummaged around, a flat box of old carbon paper caught my attention. I marveled at the obsolescence of so many tools and materials that used to be essential to writers. I opened the box to see if it looked like what we used to have around the house—my father occasionally used it.

I lifted the sheet and noted the faint image of letters and words, backward. I turned the paper over and held it up to the bright window.

I began to read the dense, single-spaced text.

Dear Miren,

I am leaving this letter with Edmond Greenwood, for him to give you when you inherit this property in accordance with my will.

I fully expect to explain my concerns to you, when next we meet, but I am writing this letter should I not get that opportunity. I am in good health for a man of seventy-nine, with the exception of being seventy-nine.

My work with Lophodermium, *which I began in the early 1960s, is recorded in my accession books and to some extent in papers published with my university colleagues Eugene Shaw, Mia Sung, and Stephen Melchior. My focus was largely on identifying new species and varieties capable of infecting commercial forests whose value lay in timber and Christmas trees.*

Two years ago, I stumbled on a valley in the Humboldt National Forest in Nevada and observed a stand of lodgepole pine that was clearly infected, with the characteristic brown needles, but the season was wrong. Normally, the needles turn brown in spring.

I collected samples and shared them with Stephen Melchior, a geneticist in the department, who confirmed my identification of an unusual variety of the fungus. Eugene Shaw, our chemist, also expressed an interest in the organism from that side of the science.

He was excited to note a structural similarity between certain of its metabolites and a class of compounds used in anesthesia. He suggested we seek a grant to fund further studies.

We were in the process of writing the proposal when Eugene told me he'd examined the spectrum of metabolites found in the fungus during its fruiting stage and found these to have even more potential as an antibiotic.

We all agreed that, from a safety standpoint, we needed to exercise great caution in the design and execution of any further study of these compounds.

Unfortunately, we lost Eugene shortly thereafter. When he died, his son, Lawrence, suffered greatly. His behavior became, in my view, unstable.

I will not elaborate on Lawrence's shortcomings in detail. Indeed, I would prefer to focus on his inner light, and I trust in time he will follow it. Until then, I feel the need to keep certain items out of his hands: the current form of the fungus, the maps that show precisely where it was collected, and the accession book for the first part of 2010.

I am setting aside a substantial amount of this material for research purposes but prefer to keep it at home rather than at the lab. I sense that Lawrence may search for it there, and, as it can be toxic in the wrong hands, I have safety concerns.

If our discovery should become commercially successful, any financial benefits would accrue to my estate. If you own the material, you would be entitled to some kind of compensation.

Thus, in my will, I specifically left the sample to you, with Lawrence as the contingent heir, as both his father and I shared in the research. However, I have recently developed misgivings about including his name although, assuming you remain in good health, this is unlikely to be a problem.

But my intention is to contact Edmond and correct this problem. I am putting the sample in a safe place and will reveal its location to Edmond at that time.

Yours with affection,
Your Uncle Elias

P.S. The pilot light on the water heater goes out quite frequently, especially when it's windy. You might want to check it from time to time and relight it with a match as needed.

Chapter Forty

From the archives of the *Bucks County Clarion*
Editor's Note
It is not Clarion policy to publish first-person articles by our staff or regular correspondents, other than occasional opinion columns. In our view, our reporters should cover the news, not be part of it. We have made an exception in the case of the special report by Miren Lassiter that follows. Lassiter is a correspondent, having left the Clarion staff last summer, but her personal involvement in this extraordinary case merits presenting it to you in her own words. Part I of the five-part series begins today.

Francis Xavier Rosenzweig
Managing Editor
****

Same River Twice

by Miren Lassiter
Clarion Correspondent

Part I

My hands were tied behind my back, so I had to pull the panel closed with my feet.

A word about the author...

Janet Poland is a transplant from the West Coast to Bucks County, Pennsylvania, where *Same River Twice* is set. She is poet, former journalist, and author of seven non-fiction books in addition to her mystery novel. She enjoys travel, writing flash fiction, and retweeting cute animal pictures on Twitter.